ALIEN
PLANET

By:

MAX HOLT

MaxHoltMedia

Published by MaxHoltMedia
303 Cascabel Place, Mount Juliet, TN 37122
www.maxholtmedia.com

The author is totally responsible for the content and the editing of this work and Max Holt Media offers no warranty, expressed or implied, or assumes any legal liability or responsibility for the accuracy of any information contained herein. The author bears responsibility for obtaining permission to use any portion of this work that may be the intellectual property of another person or organization.

Cover design by: Max Holt Media

ISBN-13: 978-0996610483

DEDICATION

Alien Planet is dedicated to my twin grandchildren, Olivia and Owen Holt. With the continuing improvements in medical technology they may actually live to see space travel to other planets become almost routine. Given their *obvious intelligence* they may become astronauts someday and be some of the first to set foot on Mars. If so, I will be smiling from somewhere far beyond there.

CONTENTS

ACKNOWLEDGMENTS
(UPDATED IN 2021)

I couldn't have finished this book without my wife's support. Sadly, Sandy died of cancer in 2018. My life is better because of her.

Thanks goes to my sibling authors, Willie Holt, Edna Holmes, Dan Holt, John Holt, and Connie Hall...all who encourage me toward excellence.

Thanks to my primary proofreader and editor, Carla Bower.

I appreciate my sons, Steve and Eddie who also helped with proof-reading.

Finally, I want to thank NASA for the inspiration to think beyond the clouds.

"Sometimes I think we're alone in the universe, and sometimes I think we're not. In either case the idea is quite staggering."

Arthur C. Clarke

Prologue

On Fire

Death waited below. Who's death it would be, Anson couldn't think about that right now. The unbearable heat and the increasing pressure were his concern at the moment. The young soldier struggled to keep his head upright; he was weighed down by the heavy helmet and the full body environmental system, necessary for their destination.

The cold weather Battle Suit was so restrictive he could hardly breathe. He looked around at his fellow warriors and realized that, like him, none were battle tested, except for SGT Fuegal, their Attack Team Leader. Some stared straight ahead and some had their eyes closed, praying perhaps. Some had a look of combat-soldier determination; clinched teeth and flared nostrils. He wondered if others had his dry mouth fear, riding the shuttle on this path to *certain* uncertainty.

The heat shield wrapped around the attack shuttle was doing its job; tiny particles of ceramic wearing away into an inferno just outside Anson's window. The resulting gravity of the rapid entry into the planet's atmosphere had them all firmly planted in their webbed seats.

He looked at the outline of the Drop Door on the floor in front of his seat. It would be only moments before the shuttle would come to a hover above this forbidding alien world. The shuttle pilot would give them just a couple of moments more to stand on the outlined footprints in the center of the floor panel and reach to the Drop Handles above their heads. They had all done this many times in the Hologram Deck Battle Simulator, but now it was going to be *real*.

A hundred other shuttles were traversing the same fiery path. Finally, with the fire outside gone, the crusty old sergeant began yelling the instructions for each soldier to do the final check of his equipment. Everyone checked his assigned battle buddy's environmental suit to ensure it was properly sealed against the lethal atmosphere below.

Helmet communications checks and laser

rifle-power verification completed their readiness. The sergeant gave the "STAND-UP" command and all ten sets of boots stepped forward onto the outlined footprints. Centering on those prints ensured the soldiers would not scrape against the door frame when their bodies dropped through the opening.

Anson and his brothers-in-arms reached overhead, gripped the activation levers and waited for the *"GO"* command form SGT Fuegal. Several were hoping that no one else could see their knees knocking.

In spite of the training, and drill after drill, Anson was caught off guard when the command came through his communications system. Without hesitation ten levers were pulled and ten doors on the bottom of the shuttle sprang open.

The drop to the surface seemed like slow motion. Immediately, the soldiers' helmet faceplates fogged over from the biting cold of this alien atmosphere. The fogged glass cleared just before Anson's feet hit the surface. All ten soldiers looked at each other, stunned. In spite of all the intelligence about this planet, and all of the training, no one was prepared for the sight before them.

Chapter 1

Federation Headquarters
Star Date 3720.1

Intelligence Division

Under-Admiral Mono checked the view panel, again. The update on the latest Probe Status Report was still not there. He should have been used to such disappointments by now; he had been the Chief of Galaxy Spiral-Arm Research for the last ten star dates. With over 50,000 active probes at his disposal, it had become an exhausting job.

Planning missions, maintaining the probes, and manufacturing new ones to replace those that never returned, was an ongoing challenge. His technical leadership had brought the probe loss-rate inside the wormholes down to four percent, per launch and retrieval. The award hanging on the wall, and the accompanying promotion, attested to the rarity of this accomplishment.

He checked the panel, yet again. This pending report had a special significance. The boss was hinging some important

7

decisions on the translation of language samples contained in the probes returning through the Galactic Four Wormhole. The Chief had heard the classified talk around the upper-level staff of the Intelligence Division; hostilities could result from the data stored in those probes. He glanced at the time again, and then touched the lower right corner of the panel. A smaller window opened, showing Colonel Jalto Baasan, speaking loudly into his communicator.

"...and I want that intel fed into the translator the moment the seven probes in the ninety-seven-eighteen group exit the hole...you got that?!" He listened for a moment. "Yeah, the old man is on my back. He said Platz needs it for some big meeting. Have the analyst feed it straight to me, no matter what time they finish."

He disconnected, laid the device on his cluttered desk and sat down in his seldom-used swivel chair. When the Admiral spoke, the colonel was startled by the unexpected interruption.

"My birthday is soon upon me, but I don't

yet consider myself old!" Before the embarrassed colonel could answer, he continued. "I got the reports from tunnels one, two and six, but those were routine missions. What I really need is the intel from Tunnel Four. I gather that the probes from Hole Four are late. I wondered why you hadn't reported. Any idea what's delaying them?"

The underling wiped his face. "Well, sir, data indicate that Tunnel Four has been oscillating outside of the computer-model predictions. I've directed the Data Group to do an algorithm update. Most likely, two of the missing probes impacted the inner wall; probably a nav-system failure based on the old programming or maybe faulty antimatter transmitters."

He hesitated. "Uh, both were in the targeted solar-system fly-by. Without additional analysis, we have no idea what happened to the third one. Its transmitter could have been damaged by the brush with the planet's atmosphere or, uh...it could been shot down by the aliens.

"But, we have enough redundancy in the recovered probes to retrieve the information you need. We've downloaded over a hundred t-bytes from the ones we've recovered; the translators are working on it now. As soon as I get the report I'll transmit it to you."

There was an awkward pause. "Col..., uh, Jal, listen, do the best you can, but this is a top priority for Platz. We've been probing that planet since I've been in the Division, and we've only deciphered...uh...what, maybe five percent of their language?"

"More like three percent, sir."

"Okay, well, it is what it is; not much we can do about that." He glanced at the Federation meeting schedule. "I've got just a half-cycle to get the info to Platz, so give it your best.

"Yes, sir."

Federation Conference Room

Silence hung over the conference room, like a quiet night one would experience alone on the Zorgonian Plain, just over the sharp peaks from the capital city. The stillness was only broken by the occasional gentle whirring of the joint-actuators in the android servers' arms and legs. None of the attendees spoke. This silent ritual was expected and practiced, as those around the table waited.

The planet Zorgon had been the headquarters of the Federation of Planets for at least fifty star dates. It was in the center of the closest spiral arm to the galaxy's massive black hole and remained the most central location to the majority of its member planets.

More importantly, it was within just a tenth of a star date from six of the galaxy's semi-permanent wormholes; all still being slowly drawn toward the central black hole's Event Horizon. Millions of star dates from now, someone would have to be concerned about the impending plunge into the black hole. But tonight, it was not on the agenda for discussion; there was a more immediate pressing matter.

Not surprisingly, most of the Federation's member planets were located along the paths and near the distant ends of those six wormholes. It was a young scientist from one of the newer multi-planet solar systems, known for the most habitable planets, who revolutionized space travel. The Federation became viable when he discovered how the precise targeted use of antimatter could stabilize these incredible transportation tunnels.

The most astounding innovation he and the research team developed was the method for creating an entry and exit vortex into a wormhole, anywhere along its path. The Federation leaders had traveled to his home planet to endow him with its highest award, honoring him for the discovery that had turned the separated solar systems and planets throughout the galaxy into somewhat of a *neighborhood* of planets.

Now, ships with antimatter transmitters could usually attain level-four or five Star Drive while transiting these portals across the vast reaches of space. As a result, more and more planets from the outer spiral arms had joined the Federation in recent star dates.

The distant solar systems in those outer spiral arms seemed to contain most of the *blue, temperate* planets; the envy of the galaxy. All but a few planets were occupied by beings of similar genetic coding.

The four quadrants of the galaxy had been divided into pie-shaped sectors, each with its own command structure. Every five star dates, the representatives from all sectors gathered, as they were doing tonight, to begin the process of welcoming new members, negotiating trade routes through the wormholes and fine-tuning the Federation laws that governed the diverse planets' and beings' coexistence. This process had served the Federation well and had negotiated myriads of planet disagreements before they could lead to hostilities.

These gatherings were also a time to deal with security threats and disciplinary actions necessary to keep all planets aligned with the Federation's purpose and goals, and to maintain the peace. It was this last task that had the Federation's leadership on edge.

Finally, the silence was broken. The Premier's entrance was announced by his android assistant, first in the Trade Language followed by the two most prominent languages in the outer spiral arms. Automatic translators, built into representatives' headsets, made multi-language reports unnecessary, but it had become *tradition*.

All representatives rose in respective silence as the Premier entered and then nodded to each group in attendance. Having seated himself, he nodded once again for the delegates to be seated and for a swarm of androids to begin serving the Zorgonian Ale that had become the staple of every official meeting.

After everyone was served, the aging leader lifted his glass and toasted to the continued harmony and cooperation of all member planets. With the formalities out of the way, the meeting was officially begun.

Finally, Premier Gaddik stood. "I bid every representative a warm welcome to Zorgon. I especially want to welcome our new members; all thirty eight thousand new planets, mostly from Quadrant Three."

The Sector leaders from Quadrant Three stood and cheered. The Premier raised his glass again, acknowledging their success in recruiting new member planets.

The Premier continued, "Whatever you need to make your stay comfortable will be provided by the androids assigned to your delegation. Please inform me if anything fails to meet your expectations."

He paused and referenced the view panel in front of him. "I have read all of the preliminary reports and agreements you sector leaders have made prior to this meeting. All of them seem to be in order and contain negotiations agreeable to the Federation." He smiled. "I noticed that Sector Three negotiated a special price for a star date's worth of Zorgonian Ale. No wonder you were able to recruit so many new member-planets."

The laughter lasted more than a few moments. The Sector Three leaders once again lifted their glasses in celebration. The android servers began bringing refills for them.

After an additional toast to Sector Three, the Premier finally got the meeting started. "Please, open File 5719-B on your panels so we can get the most pressing matter resolved first. Most of you know that Admiral Platz has been leading the Federation's Intelligence Division for some time now. Some may not know that he is from one of our more temperate member planets and that he finds Zorgon a little on the cool side for his tastes. That accounts for the cloak you see over his uniform." Some attendees laughed.

The leader continued. "Of course, the Admiral's recent report is what he feels all of us should be the most concerned about." He turned to his left. "Admiral, update us on the details and explain what is driving your level of concern."

Admiral Platz was well-respected throughout the galaxy for his skill in both combat and politics. He had started his Federation service as a Combat Commander and had later been promoted to be the Federation's Intelligence Chief, when the headquarters moved to Zorgon all those star dates ago. But he enjoyed being with soldiers and stayed active in combat operations as often as possible.

With his political hat on, he had negotiated well with those members who resisted the expansion of the Federation's fleet of interstellar probes. His financially-controversial upgrade of the probes, to make them wormhole capable, was now seen as a feather in his cap. Without life-forms onboard, the probes were now able to attain level-three Star Drive in open space and an unheard-of level-ten inside the tunnels. Those multi-light-speeds supported the belief that the Galaxy was indeed becoming a 'small world.'

The new high speed capability of the probes enabled the Federation to gather intelligence about planets scattered throughout even the most distant solar systems and planets in the galaxy. And, it was the probes returning through the Galactic Four Wormhole that had confirmed Admiral Platz's concern that now led *to the recommendation he was about to make.*

The Admiral cleared his throat. "Fellow Federation members, you may recall our last meeting, where I shared a worrisome fact with you. Probes sent to the outer reaches of Quadrant Four had detected the presence of refined atomic material on one of the inner planets of star system 4117-Alpha. We all know the violent history of most of our planets; how we each had to go through the atomic stage and almost be destroyed before finally ridding ourselves of that destructive material." He paused for a sip of ale.

"I have several concerns about this rogue planet. First, it is a moderately temperate planet, similar to here on Zargon, but with some zones much colder. Its inhabitants are far behind the evolution of virtually every other similar planet, even my own.

"You all know that, up to this point, we have catalogued over a hundred million blue temperate planets in our galaxy. Many of you are from such planets, and you would be surprised how primitive this species is, compared to all others we have encountered.

"Secondly, they not only possess raw atomic material, but they have long-ago started refining the material and developing weapons based on its explosive nature. The sad history of my own planet reveals well the destructive nature of such weapons. Many of my species actually died from the misguided use of them. But that was eons ago; just a faint memory in history. Many of you have similar stories. But, this planet is actively developing greater and more-lethal atomic capabilities."

A Third Class General from the second galactic arm spoke into his translator. "But Admiral, I don't mean to sound harsh or unconcerned, but is it really our job to police every nonmember planet in the galaxy? Many planets have their own weapons development research. And all of us had to learn from the mistake of experimenting with atomic material. Why not just leave them to their own devices and let them sort it out?"

Other delegates were nodding their agreement.

"Well, General, you have asked the

logical question. And, that is a good lead-in to my greatest concern. Just in the last few time-cycles, probes returning from that sector have confirmed that this planet has mounted those weapons on primitive spacecraft and launched them out of their atmosphere. We assume they are testing their ability to transport them to other planets in their solar system.

"My analysts have studied all probe reports carefully and now believe that it is only a matter of time before these creatures develop the capability to travel beyond their own solar system. While we don't know what their intentions would be, we can all see the potential danger of a primitive species entering other solar systems with live atomic weapons on board their ships.

"I and my staff have analyzed all pertinent data and brain-stormed the options. So, understanding what we know, I am prepared to recommend a course of action for the Federation."

Several members stood, indicating their desire to ask questions. The Admiral recognized a representative from System 1152-B. He displayed obvious concern as he spoke.

"Admiral, surely you have sent a communications probe to open a dialogue with the species in question. How did they respond to your inquiries about their intentions?"

The meeting paused as Admiral Platz touched his view panel and spent a few moments reviewing the screen. He finally looked up. "I wish it were that simple, but it is actually quite complicated. The problem stems from the fact that even though there are over a thousand different species at this meeting, this alien species is entirely different from all of us here.

"Our probes have been gathering language samples from their planet, going back ten star dates. My Translation Division has been working diligently with our latest data processing systems..." he paused, "...but the best they have been able to do is about a three percent translation."

The delegates couldn't believe what they

were hearing. One called out. "Only three percent?! Surely not!"

The admiral continued. "I know it sounds strange, but this alien language is the most complicated we have encountered. The most recent probe mission suffered a thirty percent loss of probes, so additional probes have been sent and we will analyze the new data when they are available. However, my experts do not hold a lot of hope that we will be able to effectively communicate with this species anytime soon. But, we will continue to work toward that goal."

Premier Gaddik leaned forward. "Admiral, I think it is time to share your recommendation about how best to deal with this potential crisis."

"Yes, Sir." The Admiral accessed a different file and projected an image onto the huge view screen hanging over the massive conference table.

"This schematic of the galaxy shows the location of the rogue planet, in the spiral arm in the same quadrant as the Galactic Four Wormhole. The Galactic Four has been fluctuating somewhat in recent time-cycles but it will be stable enough for us to use for the next five star dates. I am proposing a mission to this planet to solve this problem before it becomes a crisis.

"I estimate that the total mission time for our three ships, including preparation, training and the travel to their solar system, would be a little less than one star date. The return trip would be the same.

"Of course, I--"

Multiple conversations erupted and several representatives stood, interrupting the Admiral. One of them shouted to be heard.

"Admiral, wait! How can you hope to negotiate with them if you have been unable to translate their primitive language?"

A seasoned Battle Commander from the far end followed with; "Excellent question! And, if you are going to negotiate, why do you need three Star Ships? If this species is so primitive, the weapons on your Flag Ship would be more than enough to protect you."

The Admiral glanced at the Premier, who

stood and spoke. "Please, be seated and allow Admiral Platz to explain."

The Admiral continued. "As I was about to say, of course I will personally lead this mission. I will take a full Translation Division analysis team and the latest equipment. Even during Deep Sleep, some senior translators will remain on duty, analyzing the latest data transmitted to us from returning probes that have additional samples this planet's language. Our hope is that, before we arrive in their solar system, we will understand enough to make our demands known."

A voice from behind him questioned. "What exactly are our demands?!"

"If we can communicate, we will demand that they stop refining their atomic raw materials and destroy the weapons they already have. In return we will offer them a non-aggression peace treaty and assist them with the technology for interplanetary travel. If they remain free of such weapons for ten star dates, we will grant them access to the in-space Trade Depots that follow the end of the Galactic Four, as it fluctuates across the Outer

Arm.

"If all is well at that point, we will allow them to join the Federation as Associate Members, until they understand how to use the technology to access wormholes with their ships. Our probes have determined that their crude ships are too fragile to withstand the stresses of wormhole travel, so we will help them with that technology as well. Once they are able to transient wormholes, we will welcome them into full membership."

The Third Class General smiled. "Your plan sounds logical and prudent. But, you have not told us why you need two more Star Ships for this mission. My combat *nose* tells me that they will be Battle Cruisers. Am I right?"

Admiral Platz knew the reaction he was about to get. He nodded. "Yes, two Alpha Class Battle Cruisers,"

Premier Gaddik had to stand to calm the representatives. "Please, just listen to the plan before you condemn it.

"Admiral, explain the options you'll have once the mission arrives."

Admiral Platz cleared his throat. "Well, there *is* the possibility…uh, a *good* possibility, that we will be unable to successfully communicate with these aliens. So, we are prepared to deploy two separate Strike Divisions, to spread out around the entire surface of their planet. We will deploy a Strike Team onto the planet's surface at every site where their weapons and atomic materials are stored and at the few sites where the raw materials are still being mined. The Federation contingent on my planet is battle-ready and has a good portion of Combat Team Leaders who have combat experience.

"Every Team will be accompanied by a Chemical Squad, armed with Quanzite Neutralizing Agent. Each Team will gain access to a site where atomic materials are detected, using as little force as possible, and protect the Chemical Squads while they neutralize all atomic material on the site. The moment that is accomplished, they will return to their shuttles and travel back to our ships in orbit."

There was stunned-silence in the room as members tried to process this startling news. Someone finally asked, "But what about our own non-aggression treaties? Won't we be violating them?"

The Premier answered. "This is a non-member planet and the circumstances warrant our action. If we do nothing, and these aliens gain access to areas were member planets reside, we could be forced to take action against them when they are much more capable of waging war.

"We are certain we can make this a surprise incursion. All research shows that their weapons are inferior to ours, which will greatly reduce casualties on both sides. Unfortunately, in every military action there are casualties; that is a given. We will ensure that every leader who has combat experience will provide the most advanced hologram tactical training for our soldiers.

"My Operations Division and Admiral Platz's Staff are prepared to provide you any information you request about this mission's details. Are there any other questions for me at this time?"

There were hundreds of questions, but the decision had been made. All knew that further discussion would be a waste of time. So, no one raised a hand.

Chapter 2

The Rogue Planet
Star System 4117-Alpha

The creature gazed into the night sky, unaware of the Federation discussions trillions of galactic-units away. He marveled at the expanse of stars, visible from his planet on this crystal clear night, as it hurled through space, a resident of the Milky Way Galaxy.

This male couldn't care less about the politics of his own planet, much less the politics of other beings that he didn't even know existed. His concern was much more practical; food on the table. That purpose had brought him out of his dwelling into the cool of the night.

So, the gangly alien gripped his crude weapon and proceeded to forge through the dark forest, hunting for his prey. His night vision capability would give him an edge in the coming encounter. He stayed within sight of the Atomic Processing Plant nearby, knowing that the increased atmospheric heating would attract the animal he sought. The two previous nights had ended in frustration, as he was outwitted by a creature on the low end of the food chain. He hoped tonight would be different.

In a few moments an odd shaped four-legged creature slowly stepped into his field of vision. As he raised his weapon to kill the animal, the night sky suddenly brightened to half daylight. The alert creature was immediately spooked and scurried away.

Disgusted, the alien looked up. The atmosphere was filled with yet another meteor shower. The hunter had been born star dates ago; a product of their species' ancient mating ritual. In the passing of time he had seen countless such foreign objects falling from the sky.

As he had navigated the complicated alien path to adulthood he had seen more and more anomalies in these frequent showers. He, like many of his kind, had noticed that some of the meteors did not incinerate completely. Yet, those foreign objects did not impact the surface of his planet; they seemed to just pass on by.

But tonight his alien brain had detected an unusual number of such objects. In recent times there had been discussions about these anomalous foreign bodies. The elders of his clan had differing theories about the strange behavior of some of the *so-called* meteors.

Clans around the planet were separated by geographical barriers and rarely cooperated together. But, representatives of all groups had built a loosely knit planet organization designed to move it toward space travel. Although some knew better, leaders of that combined group had assured inhabitants that the meteors in question were not of alien origin.

Chapter 3

The Training

General Dayson's corner office was on the twenty-seventh floor of her planet's Federation Training Division Complex. The facility was perched on the side of the third largest mountain on the planet and had a perfect view of the lake cradled in the valley below, with two rivers merging into it. The view was stunning and always had a calming effect on all who could see it from the building.

But, today there was nothing calm about the atmosphere in the headquarters. The unusually quiet and otherwise routine day had been shattered, like the coffee cup the general had just thrown at the view panel on the wall near her desk. The scattered pieces were still settling on the floor as the outer office staff saw her stand with her hands on her hips, *not a good sign, they knew,* and walk toward the object of her anger, on the video panel.

General Kate Dayson was feared and respected by all who had served with her, even some of her superiors. She had an unrelenting work ethic and expected those in her command to have the same. That personal trait had served her well in the Military Academy, chosen by her at age 12 in lieu of the traditional educational route most of her peers had taken. Years later, few were surprised that she was the Honor Graduate, scoring higher in all categories than anyone in the history of the Academy.

As Honor Graduate, she was given her choice of assignments. So, as a new Under Lieutenant, she chose to command a Combat Platoon in the Outer Sector Patrol Division.

Not long after her arrival, a disgruntled planet challenged the Federation's ownership of the Sector's largest Communications Relay Station. Kate's Platoon was sent to negotiate with the rogue force and quell the unrest. Arriving at the relay station, she quickly read the signs of an ambush and initiated a quick reaction attack, securing the station after just a short battle. Only two in her Platoon were wounded; she was one.

The laser cut from her nose to the left side of her mouth took months to fully heal. She refused the normal scar treatment, opting to keep the disfigurement as a reminder to her troops of the price of peace.

She was also one of only three combat commanders who had the distinction of having traveled through all six galactic wormholes. Throughout her career all across the galaxy, her brash personality and the distinctive wound, had acquired for her the nickname, 'Scarface,' spoken only by brave souls in secret.

Two star dates earlier she had overheard a young office courier utter that name. The poor demoted soldier had not been heard from since then; he was still serving an unlimited tour on guard duty for an ore-mining operation on the most distant planet in Quadrant Three.

Kate's combat skills and ability to 'think on her feet' served to propel her quickly to the highest Combat Division rank: Under General. When the commander of her planet's Federation Training Division retired she was promoted to full General, over several other combat commanders, and given the job.

Now, she was in a video conversation with Under Admiral Volog, Admiral Platz's right-hand man. Admiral Platz had just arrived from Federation Headquarters and was having new orders issued to all commands for a mission that General Dayson was not prepared for. As the 'messenger,' Admiral Volog became the focus of her anger.

Those in the outer office waited for the reaction that always followed the crashing sound of whatever the General had thrown against the wall. Through the glass partition they could see she was now standing within a breath of the view panel. They all heard clearly when she began to yell.

"IS PLATZ OUT OF HIS MIND?!"

She had just heard Under Admiral Volog deliver the message from the Operations Division, communicating Admiral Platz's decision to dispatch a combat mission to a distant rogue planet.

The Under Admiral was momentarily

taken aback. He had heard about her fits of anger but was not prepared to be the object of one. On his end of the connection, her move toward the camera filled his panel screen with a close-up view of her flushed face and the bulging scar. It took a moment to recover command of his tongue.

"General Dayson, ma'am, I am merely forwarding the message as ordered. The purpose of the Training Division is to keep Federation soldiers ready for whatever contingency that may--"

"LISTEN, *Under* Admiral! Don't tell me what my job is! I am intimately aware of the mission of the Training Division."

The object of her anger was wiping his face. "Please, General, just remember that Admiral Platz has the greatest confidence in your division's ability to fine-tune our combat units for such a mission. After all, he was the one who recommended you for this job."

Kate stepped back an arm's length and studied Admiral Volog for a moment. He was still wiping the sweat from his face. The stern look on her face gave him little comfort during the brief pause. Finally she spoke, her volume beginning to slowly increase with each statement.

"Okay, I understand you are just the messenger, but as the Acting Commander of Operations you are certainly aware of the most recent Personnel Status Report. Did you inform the Admiral that our contingent of the Federation's Attack Divisions is only at seventy percent strength and that the most recent graduating class from the Academy is the only one in the last star date?!"

She paused to calm down. "Is he aware that it would take me one whole Star Date to get our inexperienced troops trained for such a mission? AND, since I heard he told the Federation that seventy percent of our leaders are combat experienced, does that mean he has forgotten that the real number is only fifty percent?!"

She had once again moved closer and closer to the view panel with each of the last few questions. The Under Admiral was nodding with each question.

"Yes, General, the Admiral is well aware

of all of your recent reports. Let me recommend that you meet with him and express your concerns in person. I'm sure he has his reasons for limiting the Federation's mission to just our forces."

"That's EXACTLY what I'll do!" Without giving him a chance to respond she disconnected from the video link and then turned to the door and called out, "JAYSON THREE!"

Jayson Manufacturing's third generation Android Server stepped through the door of her office with a fresh cup of coffee in hand.

"Excuse me General, I thought you might like some fresh coffee, since it seems you have dropped your cup...again." There was a hint of a smile on his android lips.

These third generation android models displayed the closest thing to human traits the industry had ever produced. DNA-type algorithms in their programming enabled each to develop a different mimicked personality. Designed to mimic a male, Jayson Three had developed what he had been referring to as a

"Sub-Human Manhood Personality."

Kate's habit of involving the androids in sporting events was controversial because it had virtually worn out the two previous android models that had been assigned to her. She had been chided by Headquarters for using them as sports partners, particularly in Combat Ball, where it was normal for a fourth of the players to end up in the Infirmary. H.Q. could live with soldiers recovering from injuries but the androids were very expensive to repair; sometimes costing over 100,000 GN. And, as her boss had pointed out, Galaxy Notes did not grow on trees.

The General returned the android's *half-smile.* "Okay, Jayson, I'll take that almost-insult, but only from you. Put the coffee on the desk and clean up this...uh...accident."

The android began the cleaning task as the General touched the Communicator on her desk, and then linked it to the View Panel before speaking Admiral Platz's name.

Division Personnel Office

Lieutenant Silas Danade looked confused and a little *lost* as he sat in the Combat Division's Personnel Assignments Office. He had already heard the term *Shave Tail* whispered by a couple of the clerks who were processing his assignment orders. He knew that they could tell he was a new graduate of the Officers' School and that this would be his first assignment as a Combat Officer.

During Officer Training, he had accumulated one of the highest numbers of STUs of Hologram Combat Training; over a thousand. But it was obvious that few in the headquarters regarded logging that many Standard Time Units in the Battle Simulator, as anything to brag about. He had already been reminded by other graduates that there were some soldiers in the Division who had more time than that in *actual* combat. Over-Sergeant Fuegal was one of those soldiers.

It was the Sergeant's background that led the Lieutenant to request command of the Sergeant's Attack Team. Other officers had also requested the same Team, so the

Lieutenant saw it as somewhat of a *coop d'état* to be approved for the position. He had no anticipation of going into combat, given the Federation-wide peace that had evolved. But, *if* the Division had a reason to go into a combat situation, Sergeant Fuegal would be the best combat-experienced leader to learn from.

The sergeant was somewhat of a legend in the Division. He had been a Corporal in General Dayson's Platoon when, as a Lieutenant, she led the attack on the Communications Relay Station all those star dates ago. When she was wounded in the face, it was Corporal Fuegal who leaped to her defense, protecting her during those moments when she was unconscious.

He took out three attackers before he was wounded in the arm. Encouraged by Lieutenant Dayson and the Corporal, the remainder of the Platoon intensified their attack and overwhelmed the rogue unit.

Since their combat interaction that day, the General had negotiated the corporal's reassignments to coincide with hers, keeping him in her dividion and fast-tracking his promotions. Being a die-hard combat soldier, Sargent Fuegal had convinced the General to allow him to continue serving in the smaller Attack Teams, even though he held one of the highest noncommissioned officer ranks in the Division.

      Finally, Lieutenant Danade was called in for his interview with the Reassignment Officer. The Colonel-in-charge welcomed him and began his orientation, which included the detailed status of the Division's forces and a description of how the Lieutenant's assigned Team would fit in with the operational training plans. Since he would be serving with Sergeant Fuegal, considered the best trainer in the Division, fifty percent of their team had been staffed with recent graduates of the Combat Soldier Training Academy.

      Half way through the orientation, the Colonel was interrupted by an incoming call on his private communicator. He hesitated as he read the identity of the caller. It was

General Dayson. He actually stood as he answered the call. He just listened and then he simply said, "Yes, General, right away." He then disconnected and sat down.

After a moment of contemplation he looked at the Lieutenant. "Uh...we'll have to cut this short. I have to go to a meeting with General Dayson." He started toward the door and then looked back. "I suggest you find Sergeant Fuegal and have him assemble your Team in not less than three time units, for a change of orders." As the Colonel exited the office he addressed his assistant. "Captain, cancel all personal leaves and recall all units from routine patrol."

After a preliminary meeting with General Dayson, Admiral Platz had called all of his Division Commanders and their staffs together for the briefing no one was expecting. They had all received the message about the Admiral's decision to lead a Federation mission to a rogue planet farther out in the galaxy. Admiral Platz spent time explaining the *why* of the mission and then addressed the operational and training requirements to make it a success. When it came time for Q&A, General Dayson was the first to stand with a question.

The Admiral smiled. "Well, Kate, why am I not surprised that you have the first question?"

Others muffled a laugh.

The General was not amused but she was respectful of her boss. "Sir, we can all understand the Federation's concern about the potential danger of a rogue planet with atomic weapons capabilities. But, even after our meeting earlier, I personally am not convinced that this requires the urgency you mentioned. However, as you know, I am a team player and will certainly support any mission assigned to me. But, I have a couple of different concerns.

"First, my staff and I already agree that, with such a large percentage of combat soldiers just graduating from Academy Basic Training, it will take at least one Star Date to bring them up to speed on the combat procedures needed for this operation. I realize that, in this case, actual combat may not be required, but in the event that it is, the attack teams must be ready to accomplish the mission with minimum losses.

"Also, we are confused as to why our planet is supplying all of the attack teams. Federation reports show that System 6422 Bravo has the most combat trained teams of any system at the moment. Why not employ some of their teams on this mission?" Kate sat down, indicating she was waiting for a reply.

The Admiral contemplated for a moment before answering. "I understand your concerns and, honestly, anyone else around this table would have asked the same question you did. I am well aware of System 6422's capabilities, but the Federation feels that it would be prudent to launch this mission in less than a third of a star date.

"The primary combat teams in System 6422 are on patrol at the outer end of the Galactic Six Wormhole. The flow of traffic through that tunnel will prevent them from being available for half a Star Date, at the earliest. So, we will have to go with our teams here.

"I know your concern is combat training. It is a *given* that you may have to shorten the training cycles. But, you are a creative leader. I feel sure you can overcome that concern."

The General sipped the water her Jayson Three had just placed in front of her. It had learned to assess her anxiety and find a way to mute her anger, especially when superiors were in the room. She nodded her approval of his action and then replied to the Admiral.

"Admiral, I appreciate your confidence in my skills, but I have yet to learn the art of working miracles. Certainly, we can cut out some of the fluff and shorten some of the procedures but there is no way I can have them combat-ready by your departure date.

"My only option at this late date would be to stay with the standard training regime. That means that the final three Standard Star Units of training would have to be completed onboard the mission ships, after they launch.

"That would mean that the Operations Division would have to agree to delay our troops' Deep Sleep for that period of time. Also, Logistics would have to plan for the additional supplies to support that much Awake Time in the tunnel. If I can get those agreements I think it is doable. Of course, I will personally accompany my Training Division contingent during the mission."

The Admiral looked at the Operations and Logistics leaders. After their nods of approval he smiled at General Dayson and extended his hand to her. "Welcome aboard!"

Chapter 4

The Arrival

Star Date 3720.9 was full of promise for the newest crop of Federation Training Academy recruits, preparing for their first real action as soldiers. They had been on a *fast-tracked* training regime since graduation.

There were rumors circulating about the mission objectives of their training and whether or not it was going to be just a practice run to assess their skills. Most of the young soldiers were not convinced that they would have to actually use what they were learning.

But, Anson Grotag had a feeling that the trainers were very serious about the potential danger they would face. Now, at home on furlough, before his first deployment, he was determined to put the coming danger out of his mind and have some fun.

The family had gathered to celebrate Anson's graduation from the Federation Training Academy and to wish him well on his pending departure and service as a *real* soldier. His mother and father were especially proud that he was the sole representative of the family in the military. His father had announced during the celebration that, upon Anson's return from his first mission, he would be presented with a Solar-Grid, Class 3 personal shuttle. His mother didn't mention that she had ordered it with the optional infant-system attachments; just in case the future turned out the way she hoped.

Anson was known in his family for his consistent display of humility, but on this day, he allowed a measure of personal pride to creep in. Because of his new status as a *Federation combat soldier* he was bragged-on and congratulated at every turn. All ten cousins had come for the special dinner, even the ones from beyond the second mountain range; two of which he had never met.

As a special surprise, his parents had paid for a video-link with his grandparents, on his father's side. As doctors, they had launched with a medical colony, in route to the planet's moon, three star dates ago. They would be helping to staff a new children's clinic, supporting the settlement established by the planet's Environmental Expansion Project ten star dates earlier. His grandparents had wanted some adventure in their older age and liked the added *plus* of living in a lower-gravity environment.

Everything was fantastic at the party; the food, the fun, the games and, of course, the gifts. Two young twin cousins had even given him the large jar of jelly candies they had gotten for their previous birthday, not knowing that the candy would spoil, long before Anson completed his time in *deep sleep* during the coming mission. He thanked them anyway and then secretly shared the treats with his older cousins and siblings.

The day was perfect, except for one thing; his sweetheart was not there. His *intended* had stayed away, allowing the family to have their special time together with their *hero.* But Anson was having difficulty keeping her out of his mind. He was already dreading the long separation to come.

On the next sunrise, Anson was already out of bed and ready to put his final plan into motion. He needed to spend as much time as possible with the love of his life. So, a day at the ocean seemed like a good place to start. He borrowed the family hoover-craft, loaded the necessary supplies and headed to her house in the city.

Finally, they were both on the way to the beach. Once there, he was enjoying the full speed chase of his beautiful Yanti as she splashed through the ocean surf, trying to outrun him back to the waiting picnic feast on the beach. Just before Anson caught her, she laughed and turned toward the sea, and then dove into a crashing wave. In only a moment Anson was wrapping his arms around her waist, lifting her out of the salty water up into a face to face hug.

As he carried her toward their towels on the beach she stared up at him with her broad smile. With one hand she wiped the water from her face and pushed her long braids back over her head.

"Well, PRIVATE, if you can't run any faster than that, how do you expect to make it in the Space Fleet? All the aliens will have to do to get away from you, is run."

Anson's smile turned into a pucker and he gave her a quick kiss. Having reached the towels he stopped and said, "Well, Missy, in the glorious history of the Fleet, there is no record of an encounter with aliens as feisty as you." With that, he dropped her onto her towel and fell down beside her. They both laughed.

As they lay back to enjoy the warmth of the sun's rays, Anson closed his eyes. He was still amazed that Yanti had been receptive to his romantic pursuits. Other than being in the same university graduating class, they had little in common, except maybe their love for the outdoors.

He was from a middle-class family in the mountain region and she was a socialite from a wealthy family in the largest coastal city. His father was a Maintenance Supervisor at the Fleet's Antimatter Engine Division.

Yanti's father, a Fifth-Class General, was

the Chief of Planet Security. He was in line to be the next Interplanetary Liaison; a representative to the Federation of Planets. Anson was glad the General's keen military mind would be in that position.

During his recent training, Anson's class had been told about the rogue planet with a super-weapon that could possibly endanger theirs and all other Federation planets. Some were skeptical that the threat was significant but everyone on the planet admired Admiral Platz. All of the citizens trusted his judgment and were quick to embrace his solution to the threat.

Actually, Anson couldn't care less about all the political aspects of such military actions. At this moment, with Yanti so close to him, he just wanted to concentrate on this amazing young female. He still had to pinch himself to believe this rich/poor relationship was working. Whatever the reason, he was glad.

The other soldiers in his squadron envied his relationship with Yanti. They all told him how lucky he was and some made jokes about how she obviously had to lower her standards to even to be seen with him. Anson enjoyed the good-natured humor, although he did actually feel that he was a little out of his league.

But he was a Fleet Soldier now and, throughout all levels of society, there was great admiration for those who wore the uniform. Besides, being the first in his family to join the Fleet, he was respected and admired, especially by the younger relatives. Anson enjoyed the attention.

However, no one knew the questions and reservations he harbored inside about the possibility of actually going into combat and engaging an alien enemy. Anson felt sure the rumors about the pending *actual combat* were true, despite the media reports that the Federation just wanted to justify more funding from member planets.

Up to this point, except for one small skirmish, the entire Federation of Planets had lived in harmony throughout the galaxy. His Attack Team had not actually had to fire their weapons in combat since that little Relay

Station attack many Star Dates ago, long before he donned the uniform, or was even born.

Only a few of the older leaders had been in that battle and were the only ones with any real experience in combat. Anson squirmed a little every time he saw the scars on those who had been wounded.

Everyone knew how General Dayson had gotten her scar. Anson had seen her several times during training but he avoided looking directly at her. He was afraid he'd get into trouble for *staring.* She didn't seem to mind the troops looking at a reminder of what it can be like in combat. Anson understood how she got the nickname, *Scarface,* but he would never be so stupid as to utter it out loud.

All of the experienced leaders in the Basic Training Regiment had reminded the recruits that no amount of hologram training could prepare them for that first face-to-face encounter with an enemy whose mission was to kill them. He had no reason not to believe it.

Anson was sure he was not afraid to fight;

he just didn't see the sense in it, at least not until all diplomatic measures had failed. Somehow he was sure there would be fewer intra-galaxy conflicts if all of the politicians had been required to serve in the military or at least in some security position on their own planets.

But, both politics and females were mysteries to him. So, he decided to just relax and enjoy this beautiful day with his beautiful Yanti and maybe catch a few winks in the warm sunshine. He felt privileged to be at such a great place in his life.

That evening would include a combination celebration of Anson's and Yanti's relationship and of his deployment on his first *real* mission as a soldier in the Federation's Fleet. He was anticipating the delicious Sargonian Chicken his mother had brought in on the most recent delivery ship arriving through the Galactic Three Wormhole. It was the most expensive meal he would ever have, but he was proud when his mother had said, *"Soldiers deserve the best."*

Suddenly, there was a rush of cold air. Anson thought it must be a variant air current, perhaps coming from the ocean. He almost opened his eyes but quickly dismissed it as a momentary change in the weather. What *did* seem strange though, was the odor that drifted on that cool breeze. It smelled a lot like... common bad breath.

Sergeant Fuegal's loud voice startled Anson as it echoed in his ears.

"HEY PRIVATE! Are you gonna sleep through the whole star date? It's time to wake up; time to be a real SOLDIER!"

Anson opened his eyes and saw the scraggly face of Sergeant Fuegal, the famous combat soldier who was now his Combat Attack Team Leader. It was immediately obvious that he was the source of the unpleasant halitosis.

Anson couldn't imagine what the crusty old soldier was doing here, on the beach. He was sure he hadn't told anyone where he was taking Yanti for some private time before the scheduled deployment.

When he attempted to put his hands up to block some of the sun's rays, he couldn't lift his arms; they felt like lead weights. Anson had to clear his throat before he could speak.

"Hey Sarge, what are you doing here? I'm on Personal Furlough; how did you find me?"

The bad-breath smile got wider. "Wake up, kid, you're deployed on Solar Two. Turn off your Chip, it's time to hit the deck. We're about to come out of the Hole."

Anson glanced over at Yanti, still asleep on her towel, and then back at the sergeant. "What?!"

The old soldier grunted. "Your Chip, Private, your Dream Chip, it's still running; turn it off."

With that, the Combat Team Leader turned and walked to the next Deep Sleep Pod.

Anson's brain was starting to return to reality. He took one last look at Yanti and then, with a sigh, he reached to the Pod Control Panel and pressed the button to deactivate his Dream Chip. Yanti, along with the beach and the ocean instantly disappeared.

He relaxed back into the soft recesses of the pod's contoured mattress, designed specifically for him. It helped make Deep Sleep on long voyages more tolerable. His whole body felt like a huge stone, ten times his normal weight. The feeling was expected and he knew he'd have to wait for his body to reactivate completely before trying to get up.

The young private closed his eyes. Yanti and the beach had seemed so real. Of course, the Chip had been designed to input predefined *realities* directly into his brain. It was the latest development by the Fleet's Medical Division to reduce the problem of memory loss during Deep Sleep on missions longer than half a star date. A glance at the chronometer showed he had been in the Pod at least that long. Including the departure sequence and the unusually long training regimen on board after departure, it meant the Fleet's Attack Squadrons had been in space for almost an entire star date.

Looking to his left, Anson saw the fixed digital display on the side panel. There was the photo of Yanti, smiling and dressed in her engagement party gown. He was still amazed that her parents had allowed it and that she had said *"yes."* They were to become united after his return from this mission—IF he returned from this mission.

He didn't notice Ganz approaching his pod and was startled by the verbal interruption of his thoughts.

"Hey, Mighty Warrior! Welcome back from dream land!"

"Ganz! Don't sneak up on me like that. What are you doing out of your pod already?"

"Fuegal brought me out early. He needed help with a Med-Alert."

"Medical alert? What happened?"

"Pod seal failure down on Deck Two; some private didn't make it. I heard on the Sergeant's communicator that Solar Three lost two pods; of course they're a much bigger ship."

During the moment of silence between them, Anson could hear the familiar sound coming from the forward section of the ship;

the whine of the Exotic Matter Generator. It expelled a continuous stream of antimatter, mixed with some forms of hybrid matter. Without it, transiting any wormhole would be impossible.

That high-pitched sound permeated the ship and confirmed they were still in the wormhole. He had been on two training missions but only one through a hole. Rumors said there were all kinds of failures that could happen, due to the mechanical stresses inside what the old-timers called the *Time Tunnel*, especially if the EMG was not properly calibrated. The Exotic Matter Generator was the only way to keep the ship safely inside the wormhole to achieve faster-than-light-speed travel.

But everyone knew about the loss of the first Quantum Class ship with two hundred soldiers onboard. Over a hundred Star Dates ago, its first-generation EMG failed and the ship inadvertently exited through the side of a wormhole, without a proper exit being generated. They were only half way to their destination.

The technical experts blamed a Quantum Back-Reaction as the most likely culprit. That led engineers to add elements of hybrid matter to the antimatter particle stream, to help stabilize the system.

The Federation Accident Report also estimated that the sudden penetration of the wall of the wormhole must have caused significant structural damage and some associated injuries; probably even some deaths. The instant loss of the transmitted data stream and the lack of any debris to analyze, made it impossible to know exactly what happened.

Some scientists theorized that the Quantum Surge could have even generated an adjacent wormhole with super light speeds approaching or even achieving Level-2 time travel. But no one knew for sure what happened to the ship and its crew. Federation sensors lost track of it as it disappeared into deep space, headed in the direction of the outer quadrant of the Genesis Star System in an adjacent galaxy.

Anson didn't want to imagine the chaos

that crew must have gone through before they eventually died. *"Maybe,"* he thought, *"they found an inhabited planet, in the future, and were able to land and survive, at least for their normal life-spans."*

A low popping noise in the bulkhead near his pod brought Anson back to the present. He knew these ships were somewhat flexible and could adapt to the changing stresses of space travel. Still, the occasional creaking of the ship's hull always caused his pulse to quicken.

Finally, he disconnected the brain interface band from his lower neck and, with a little struggle, he sat up and gripped the exit handle. When his other hand touched the flexible pod seal he wondered what had happened to those dead soldiers; did they feel anything or was it a quick death. He didn't know how they would notify their families.

Electronic signals would not follow a meandering wormhole. Researchers had been somewhat successful in developing

Quantum Communications; electronic transmissions that use connections across the fabric of space to communicate instantly with any other system in the Universe. The engineers were having some limited success but they were at least a star date away from testing such systems in space.

So, for now all transmissions to Home Base would have to go normal speed through open space. It would take much more than a Star Date to inform headquarters about anything. All of this was scary to Anson; not a good sign just coming out of Deep Sleep.

He looked up at his best friend. "Did you know any of the ones who died?"

Ganz sat down on the side of the pod. "Nah. It's just one of those things—they told us these missions could be dangerous. It could have been one of us. The bottom line; we are just fragile carbon-based life forms playing around out here where no life form is designed to be. Stuff happens."

He then pointed at Yanti's image on the pod display. "You know, she's over a Star

Date away, through the Hole. You may as well turn that off and try to forget about home until you get yourself straight. How's your head?"

Anson reached up and rubbed his forehead. "Just barely a hint of pain; I guess the pre-meds worked. How about you?"

"No problems. I'm *fit to fight,* as they say."

Anson activated the Shut-Down Sequence, swung his legs over the side and stood. He exercised with a few squats to get his balance. The lighted panels inside the pod shut off one-by-one and the glass canopy slowly closed. From down the row of sleep pods, they both heard Sergeant Fuegal's loud gravelly voice echoing off the walls.

"OK, WARRIORS, UP AND AT EM'! DO YOUR HYGIENE THING AND FILL YOUR BELLIES. REPORT TO THE BATTLE DECK WHEN YOU HEAR THE ANNOUNCEMENT. GO! GO!"

Both young soldiers hurried to their storage units on the bulkhead wall, retrieved their hygiene kits and joined the others headed toward the stairs. The passageway led aft to the huge open Battle Deck and past the attack shuttles that would take the teams into battle. A hundred shuttles lined both walls of the massive training deck, the place where they would rehearse landings and deployment onto the alien planet. Neither soldier wanted to think about their coming first combat experience, facing an enemy alien life-form. It was better not to talk about it, just yet.

Arriving in the cramped Hygiene Chamber they undressed and stepped into their individual cubes. High pressure liquid sprayed from all surfaces, helping return Anson's body temperature back to normal from the lowered temp of his sleep pod.

He closed his eyes and directed the spray to his face. Feeling the sting of the spray on his skin, he thought again of Yanti and how the sea spray had covered them as they frolicked in the surf a Star Date ago. Now, she was still back there, planning for the ceremony that would unite them upon his return, and he was... here.

"Why exactly am I here?" he asked

himself.

With his eyes closed against the spray, he remembered how the Federation Fleet Recruiter had come to the university and addressed his graduating class. The Fleet always sent recruiters to all universities just prior to graduation, to fill the ranks vacated by soldiers who had finished their time of service. The Recruiter reminded them of the history of the Federation; how the Fleet had played a crucial role in uniting the entire galaxy into a peace-loving organization of planets.

In a moment of patriotism, when the recruiter called for volunteers, Anson had stood as the first in his class to join the Fleet. He had decided before hand not to volunteer but he got caught up in the cheers of encouragement from the other classmates, especially Yanti. So, he stood and received the accolades of his fellow graduates. His father had been proud and his mother had shown concern, as mothers most often do when their offspring make the transition into real life.

Now, he was billions of stellar units away from home, inside a ship transiting the Galactic Four Wormhole. The mission ships were being *sucked along* inside the tube, much faster than the speed of light by an incredible level-four Star Drive. Soon they would pop out just a short Solar System distance from an alien enemy.

At least he was with his best friend Ganz and a couple of new friends he had made during training. Borta and Sardo were both from a neighboring town in the mountains. But Anson had never seen two such opposites.

Borta was mild-mannered and caring and was a natural selection for the Medical Section of their team. On the other hand, Sardo was a gung-ho soldier who had honed his combat skills during training. He had placed first in Combat Tactical Laser Targeting, which led to his bragging about being a *killing machine*.

Borta had been on the university's Political Debate Team while Sardo got awards in most of the physically challenging sports. They were exact opposites.

The liquid shower spray suddenly stopped. Simultaneously, the onboard warning system activated. Yellow lights throughout the ship began flashing. Everyone knew what was about to happen, so they looked for the nearest handhold. The computer voice rang into every compartment on the ship.

"Prepare for exit! Prepare for exit!"

Anson grabbed a towel, quickly dried off and wrapped it around himself. When the red light came on, he gripped the handhold on the cube wall with both hands. He closed his eyes and tried not to think about the Genesis ship, lost in space eons ago. With his heart fluttering he hoped that the computer systems and the EMG on Solar Two were functioning properly.

The female voice coming from the speakers counted down from 10. At the sound of *"zero"* the ship lurched into several left and right partial rolls and then felt as if it had hit a wall. The Fleet had exited the wormhole. In spite of his grip, Anson was almost slammed into the wall. His arms ached from the pressure of holding himself upright. Based on sounds coming from other cubes, it was also evident that some of his fellow warriors had not properly prepared for the exit. Anson did not remember the exit maneuver ever being this dramatic.

All four huge Antimatter engines had been reversed and were now creating miniature Black Holes behind the ship. The *sucking* action of the Black Holes was working, attempting to pull the ship backward to fill the super-vacuum voids, thus, creating the braking action needed to slow the ship's forward speed.

The initial rapid deceleration lasted only a few moments and then settled into a constant of one and a half gravity units. The ship's Gravity Generator would be adjusted to compensate, so it wouldn't last long. The new gravity would still apply some added pressure until the ship had slowed to Level One Star Drive.

Suddenly the electrical system failed, only to come back on moments later. The ship's penetration of the Solar System's Bow Shock

Wave had caused the momentary failure. The event just added to Anson's apprehension about the whole mission. He glanced at the structure all around him, half expecting something else to go wrong. After a few moments he shook off the concern and finished dressing. He opened the door just as Ganz looked into his cube. His best friend's characteristic smile made him feel better.

Ganz looked him up and down and chuckled. "Well, even Yanti might approve of your smell; maybe not your looks but at least the smell."

Anson smiled back. He needed the levity. He wondered if the aliens they were going to attack enjoyed humor as part of their culture or if they were stoic creatures as most in the Federation believed. Either way he didn't believe that they, or the Fleet soldiers, would be smiling when, or *if*, the attack finally started.

He was still holding out hope that the massive translation computers onboard would be able to decipher the aliens' complicated language. That would enable Admiral Platz to negotiate with them. Maybe they would accept the Federation's demands to destroy their weapons and everyone could avoid a confrontation.

But, rumor had it that Fleet Intelligence was unable to translate any significant amount of the language used by these strange life forms. Anson knew they couldn't possibly negotiate if they couldn't understand each other.

Together, the two friends headed toward the dining area. The long sleep period in the Pod had left them both famished. Just after entering the passageway along the outside hull of the ship Ganz stopped.

"Look at that." He was pointing out of a porthole window at numerous shuttles headed toward Solar One. The three Fleet ships had maneuvered into closer formation since exiting the wormhole. "There must be at least twenty shuttles headed over to Solar One."

Anson nodded. "When we passed the Lieutenant back there I heard him telling Sgt. Fuegal that he was going over for a meeting. All Combat Team Leaders have been called to

Solar One for a briefing with the big-wigs. You know, Admiral Plaze always gives a pep talk before any operation under his command."

Ganz nodded. "That makes sense. They're probably gonna discuss the attack. I know that Scarfa--, oops, I mean General Dayson is going to personally supervise the final Holodeck Training. I heard she is ranting and raving because the Intel Division hasn't incorporated the holograms of the alien life-forms into the training yet. They're supposed to give us at least a clue about how they look and what we'll be up against on the surface. I'm sure the LT will tell us the details later, on the Battle Deck."

Ganz paused for a moment. "But I wonder, if they are going to Solar One for a meeting, why didn't they just beam over? Seems like a waste of fuel to me, using all those shuttles."

They continued walking toward the Dining Compartment. Anson offered his opinion. "I'm not sure exactly. But when we studied the Transporter System in Basic Training I remember one of the instructors saying that the Beaming Pulses require so much energy that they are detectable at great distances. Maybe the Admiral doesn't want to take any chances that the Fleet might be detected too early."

"Yeah, I can see that. But, all that stuff is way above my pay level. Besides, we're just the lowly grunts here. Our job is to aim and squeeze the trigger, right?"

Anson shuttered a little. "Right, just cannon fodder."

Ganz smiled. "Except for Borta."

"What do you mean?"

They stopped and moved to the side of the passageway. Ganz leaned in close. "This isn't official but I heard SGT Fuegal say that Borta filed for Conscientious Objector status right after we came out of Deep Sleep."

"What?! Are you sure?"

Ganz nodded. "I'm pretty positive. Fuegal brought him out of his pod early too, to help with the Med-Alert, since he's on the Medical Team. The Sarge got ticked off because of some weird dreams Borta said he had during Deep Sleep. He says they were extra dreams that were not originally on his Chip. He said that it was some sort of *omen* that he is not supposed to take up arms against another species.

"He said something about his principles no longer allowing him to fire a weapon in combat. But all medical soldiers carry small belt weapons for their own protection. I'm not sure what they are going to do with him during the attack. He'll have to go with us. We have to have a full Medical Team on the surface."

Anson was still in shock. He thought Borta was friend enough to have mentioned his reservations earlier, during the initial on-board training cycle. Sure, he had the lowest combat scores in Basic Training but he didn't say anything about refusing to fight, although Anson had to admit that he had seen some signs of Borta's concerns.

Thinking back, he realized that his friend hadn't been a gung-ho soldier from the very beginning of his enlistment. But something significant must have happened in his Deep

Sleep pod for Borta to make such a rash decision.

"Let's not be too hasty before we talk to him. Maybe the whole thing is just a misunderstanding. When we see him, don't mention what I said about being cannon fodder."

"Okay." Ganz smiled and slapped his best friend on the back. "Speaking of fodder, I'm hungry; let's go eat."

Chapter 5

Aboard Solar One

Admiral Platz finished reading the Exit Status Report and then looked up at his War Staff, gathered around the conference table on Solar One, his Flag Ship. They had already read it and were waiting for his comments and instructions. He had only experienced one other wormhole exit as rough as this one, so he was somewhat concerned. The Fleet had lost only a few ships over the eons; just one inside a wormhole. He did not want to be the next one. But, not wanting to show his *uncertain side* he smiled at the Engineering Officer.

"Captain Sull, I trust all three of our ships are still in one piece, after that, uh...*exciting* exit from the Galactic Four. Is there anything I need to be concerned about?"

The Captain had all of the data displayed on his panel. "No sir, I don't think so. It looks like the Federation sensors did not detect the rapid expansion of this solar system's Bow

Shock Wave. The leading edge of the wave was closer to the end of the wormhole than we expected; that's why we temporarily lost electrical power so quickly after exiting. Our ships are designed to withstand such an impact but the double stress of both events can be unsettling. It did actually cause a few minor failures, such as a ruptured pressure line on Solar Three and an environmental system leak on Solar Two. I'm not concerned, because we have had such failures just from the rigors of normal space travel. Both failures are being repaired as we speak."

General Dayson offered her observation. "Well, as the most seasoned *hole traveler* on this mission I can agree with the Admiral. This was also the roughest exit I have ever experienced."

The Admiral nodded. "Yes, it was rough for all of us. We'll need to make sure we can get these *big metal tubes* back through the hole when this little, ah ...*confrontation* is over. Captain, keep me updated on any other failures."

As the Captain made a note, the aging

fleet leader turned to the Medical Officer. "Well, Doctor, how many condolence messages will I have to send when we get back home?"

The Medical Officer tried to maintain a positive demeanor. "Three, sir. We lost a Corporal and a Private on Solar Three and a Private on Solar Two. The two privates died from Pod Seal failures and the Corporal's Environmental System had a valve malfunction. The Environmental Team is investigating and should have a report soon."

The doctor saw the Admiral's stoic stare and decided he'd better embrace a little sadness. "These are tragic losses for all of us. They were brave warriors who will be missed by their comrades and their families. We will get to the bottom of these failures and work to eliminate them in the future."

The Admiral stared for a moment. "Well, you'd better; we have to go back through that hole after this is over and I don't want my Deputy having to write such a letter to my family; understood?"

The doctor was sweating now. "Yes sir.

My Division will work with Maintenance to do a thorough analysis and get back to you."

An Attack Squadron Commander stood. "Admiral, has the Intel Cipher System made any headway, translating the alien language? We still have time to negotiate with them if we can make any sense out of what they are saying."

The Intelligence Chief looked at Admiral Platz and stood. "If I may sir, my briefing will answer that question."

The Admiral nodded.

Intel continued. "Up until we discovered this alien language, the most difficult one we had encountered was of the mountain creatures on the fifth planet in the 4263D Star System, far out in the Third Quadrant. It took a Level Four language computer almost a Star Date to decipher it down to a basic communication level.

"We've had a Level Four working on this rogue planet's language for right at two Star Dates, including our time in the wormhole. So far, we've only made sense out of a tiny percentage of it; not enough to even say an intelligent *"hello."* The algorithms are very complicated. The only thing we know for sure is that the alien males and females have what seem to be separate derivatives of their common language."

The Admiral and most of the commanders burst out laughing. He recovered slightly and said. "Well, welcome to the Universe! I don't think a Level Four could even figure out what most of the females in my family are trying to say." As the rest of the Staff tried to hold back their snickering, he realized General Kate Dayson was still at the table.

He blushed as he looked at her. "Kate, I meant no offense. It's just that—"

She interrupted him. "Admiral, in most circumstances I would view such comments as just a holdover from eons ago when Male Chauvinism was at its height.

"However, I hate to admit this, but I agree with you, in this case. Although I personally have never had this problem, I do find that the male and female soldiers in my training cycles seem to have difficulties understanding each other, especially in nonverbal communications.

"Fortunately, I have trained the female Attack Team leaders to be forthright in their instructions to their units. We can't have such confusion in combat operations. So, no offense taken, sir."

The Admiral nodded and turned to the Intelligence Division Language Specialist. "Alright, continue working on the translation and we will hope for the best. But," he looked around at all of the Combat Team Commanders, "...our Federation orders require us to invade and neutralize those weapons on schedule, regardless of our language limitations. During final training, don't allow this uncertainty to deter your soldiers from preparing to do what must be done. Is that clear?"

It was, and they all nodded.

The Shuttle Protection Squadron commander had just been promoted to High Colonel and was here on his first deployment with the Fleet. Admiral Platz had personally requested him because of his fighter pilot experience in the last war and his meteoric rise through the Fleet aviation ranks.

He was a shrewd tactician and always flew in the first attack wave with his best pilots. He had already expressed some concern that his small squadron of one hundred fighters would be scattered out around this alien planet to protect the troop shuttles from air and ground fire. He was sure he could pull it off, but he'd rather not have his coverage thinned out so much. He stood to do his report.

"Admiral, and my fellow commanders, the Protection Squadron stands ready to make sure all of you make it safely to the surface when the attack begins and that you return to your hangar bays intact. We will do what is necessary to protect you." He addressed the Admiral's Combat Operations Staff Officer. "General Wu, as you know, the strength of this planet's magnetic field exceeds Level Three, which will render our shuttles' shield generators useless. So, my pilots will have to rely on good old fashioned combat tactics. Can you give us the latest data on the alien aircraft weapons capabilities?"

The General had prepared a schematic of

the known alien weapons systems. He spoke as his assistant pointed them out on the view panel. "The bad news is; there are thousands more combat-type aircraft on this planet than we brought with us, which means that you will be out-numbered.

"The good news is; their weapons and target acquisition developments are far behind just about every other planet in this quadrant of the Universe, at least, all of the Federation planets. Their aircraft are slower and more fragile than our smallest shuttles and, at least so far, our probes have not detected more than just a few aircraft weapons tests above their atmosphere. So, we believe that the potential danger to troop shuttles lies completely inside their atmosphere.

"Therefore, I recommend that your Protection Squadron fighter shuttles deploy at least fifteen Standard Time Units ahead of the troop shuttles so they'll be under your protection the moment they complete atmosphere penetration. The planned stealth entry and the steep approach to the surface should reduce their exposure to alien detection and counter-attack.

"The most likely locations of their fighter aircraft have been fed into your attack computers, so your detection systems should already be aimed at those areas. Data from all returning probes have shown no indication that these enemy aircraft have shields of any kind. I assume they have the same problem as we do with the magnetic field. I believe these facts and our preparations could keep our losses under five percent, maybe even down to one percent."

The Admiral chimed in. "It looks like we have the edge, especially in the atmosphere. But my main concern is for our troops when they hit the surface. They do not yet know that they're going to be fighting in cold weather bio-suits and we all know how cumbersome those can be. A few STUs from now, after all troops have been fed, the hologram battle training will begin on the Battle Deck.

"While we were in the Hole the Intel simulators knitted together a hologram of the most likely alien soldier our troops will face.

We believe it to be over ninety percent accurate. I want all of you to see it before the troops do, so you can reassure them of their capability to defeat these creatures."

The Admiral nodded to the Intel Chief, who activated the hologram generator in the ceiling, over the conference table. In a few moments a full sized three dimensional image of an alien from the target planet appeared just above the table, slowly rotating. Even the experienced combat veterans in the room were stunned. Some of the younger leaders recoiled slightly from the depiction but quickly recovered. The alien was huge and ugly. The multiple appendages and orifices coupled with the giant head made it even more grotesque.

Admiral Platz stood and walked closer to the image. "It's clear why I wanted you to see this image first. Our troops may not understand how superior our weapons and fighting skills are, compared to this gross entity. In many ways these creatures are still in the stone age; almost as crude as when our species lived in caves and used clubs eons ago. There is still a lot about this planet and these aliens that we do not know. Your job is to lead our troops to focus on what they *do* know and to use that knowledge to accomplish the mission."

He looked around the room in silence before speaking again. "You are the finest leaders the Federation has to offer. You lead the best trained and motivated fighting force I have had the privilege to command. Prepare them well for this mission and bring them...all of them, back alive. Operations will download to your Battle Simulators the holograms of the aliens and their planet. Intelligence will continue our translation efforts and you will be informed the moment any success is realized. Good luck! You are dismissed."

Chapter 6

Soldiers

The meal had been fantastic; just what Anson needed to revitalize his body and his spirit. Leaving Ganz talking with some other soldiers he made his way to the Troop Housing Module and entered the hot cramped quarters.

He squeezed past a maintenance crew working to replace a defective bypass valve in the environmental system. Anson assumed that it was caused by the rough exit from the wormhole. He walked slowly down the passageway between the rows of sleep cubicles, looking for Borta. His friend had avoided him during their first meal after Deep Sleep. He figured Borta had probably eaten with the medical unit, just to avoid the awkwardness of discussing his decision to file a request to be considered a conscientious objector.

Anson had no plans to berate that decision; honestly, he had some of the same reservations. There was a nagging question inside him about the *why* associated with the coming attack on these aliens. After all, it was not like they had overtly threatened the Federation. No one had even successfully communicated with this species yet. But regardless, he was ready to do his duty. His father had taught him that the mission always had to come first if a free society was to remain free. Still, he needed to hear Borta out, to understand why he had made the decision. He wouldn't try to change his friend's mind unless he felt an opening to do so.

"You're looking for me, right?"

Anson turned to see Borta following him. "Borta, I missed you at meal time and just wanted to see how you were, coming out of your pod."

"I was exhausted. It took a while to recover. Helping with that dead soldier didn't make things any better. I'm still a little woozy but, I'm guessing that's not all you really wanted to talk about." He motioned to his cramped cubicle nearby. "Come in and you can get right to the point."

Anson followed him in and sat by his friend on his bunk. "You're right; I heard you had filed a request for C.O. with the Lieutenant right after coming out of Sleep. But I don't go much for rumors so I thought you could fill in the details for me."

Borta had been looking down. He lifted his head and stared at Anson for a moment. "It's true, I filed. It was the dreams."

"The dreams? In Deep Sleep?"

Borta nodded.

"But you designed your own Chip, right? I mean, surely the dreams were just the ones you downloaded before departure."

Borta was shaking his head. "There was an additional one that kept creeping in. Right in the middle of a family vacation sequence or during the graduation party this same dream would pop into my head out of nowhere."

Anson was shocked. "How is that possible? Your Dream Chip transmits directly into the basic nervous system. It is designed to overpower all other subconscious thoughts."

"Don't ask me. All I know is that the

message must have been strong enough to get through."

"Get through? What do you mean; get through from where?"

Borta looked up. "I don't know; it's really strange."

"Okay, tell me the dream."

His friend swallowed hard and his skin became clammy from a pre-sweat. "The dream was always the same and repeated itself more times than I can remember. It starts out with our Battle Team on the shuttle hovering over the surface of an alien planet, the one we're going to I guess.

"The green Drop Light comes on and the Sarg yells for us to go. It seems like slow motion as the ten of us drop through the doors and land on the surface. The vegetation is so thick that I can't see any of you.

"Laser blasts start coming from everywhere. The smoke and mist from the lasers are hot and stifling and I can't seem to move faster than a crawl. Immediately all of you are gone and I'm alone, not knowing which way to turn. My helmet communicator isn't working and even though I'm wearing my survival system I'm finding it harder and harder to breathe.

"Finally I hear low frequency screeching noises all around me and somehow there's an awful smell penetrating my respirator, an odor that can only be coming from aliens.

"Then, there is the loud cracking sound of a tree breaking behind me. As I turn around my feet get caught in some sort of vegetation and I fall flat on my back.

"I look up and there, standing over me, is the most horrid sight; an alien three times my size, with a distorted body and a huge head. It is the ugliest thing you can imagine. It raises some sort of long pointed weapon and aims it at me. My heart is pounding and I'm sure that I'm about to die.

"But, it just stands there, motionless. I realize that my laser rifle is still in my hand so I raise it to an aiming position with the alien's huge head in the sights. Before I can squeeze the trigger the alien drops its weapon, spreads both of its long gangly arms into the sign of a cross and just stands there smiling at me. I try to pull the trigger but my finger is powerless; I can't make it move.

"The next thing I know, the shuttle comes over the trees and hovers right above me. By then there are several aliens standing over me. They all drop their weapons and lift me off the surface and up through the door and into the shuttle. The shuttle departs and I look back out through the window. All of the aliens are smiling and waving. Finally the dream ends, only to be repeated again in the middle of some other Dream Chip sequence."

Borta wiped his face and glanced up at Anson. "It was almost like…"

Anson hesitated. "Like what?"

"Almost like the aliens were warning me through my dream."

Anson just stared at Borta, not knowing what to say. He had never heard of such dreams overriding a Dream Chip, and he could not imagine the aliens being the source. He felt sure they didn't have that kind of technology. But he could tell that Borta wasn't lying about the details of the dream. Finally he asked, "What do you think it means?"

Borta was taking a drink to help him recover from his first verbal description of the awful dream. "I think it means that this attack is a mistake. I think those aliens want to live in peace as much as we do. They care about life and they mean us no harm. I think all this business about planet-destroying weapons is just hype. It's probably just an excuse for the Federation to spread its political power further out in the Universe. I've decided that I can't be a part of it."

Anson just stared at him, trying to think of a response. He finally said, "Listen, soldiers like us don't have the authority or clout to get this attack stopped. I don't think the Intel guys are any closer to communicating with this species than when we entered the Hole. I doubt seriously if any negotiations will ever take place.

"So, whatever we do, some of us will end up dropping through those exit doors onto the surface. And when we do, you medical types will become very important. Surely you're not going to stay here in your cube while we drop into the unknown."

Borta sat up straight, a little offended. "Of course not! I'm not a coward! I'll be right there on one of the Med-Drop Teams. But, I've told the Medical Tech that I refuse to carry a weapon on the surface. I'm convinced that no alien would harm me if it can see that I am unarmed."

"Suppose you're wrong?"

Borta thought for a moment and then smiled. "If I'm wrong, tell my family that I love them and that I did what I thought was right."

Anson reached out his hand and smiled as Borta gripped it. "Well, I can't ask for more than that."

They talked for a little longer, with Anson finding ways to take the conversation toward less controversial subjects. Finally the alert tone sounded, signaling it was time to gather their gear for their first training session on the Battle Deck.

Anson stood. "Don't worry about Ganz and Sardo, I'll straighten them out about how you feel. There may be a little ribbing from some of the team, but you can handle that."

They both secured their training bags and made their way to the Battle Deck, with a thousand other soldiers.

MAX HOLT

Chapter 7

Preparations

On all three ships, the squadrons were very impressive, arrayed in Attack Team formations, covering the gigantic floor of each Battle Deck; their training area for the next eight alien planet rotations. The hundred attack teams on Solar Two, plus the same on Solar One and the three hundred teams on Solar Three would be a formidable force for the aliens to reckon with, or so Admiral Platz assured everyone.

The plan was to attack only those sites where probes had detected the atomic signature of the weapons, stockpiled in locations around the planet. The truth was that no one was sure the Fleet's force was enough to get into the storage sites and neutralize the aliens' powerful weapons. But the Admiral had said to his leaders that sometimes, *"You have to go with what you have and trust that you've done your homework."*

All combat leaders had also heard the

alert tone coming from the shipboard broadcast system. Admiral Platz's voice then directed all leaders to begin their attack training.

On Solar Two, Lieutenant Danade acknowledged the command. He gathered his Attack Team around the portable video unit provided for their final training. He had reviewed the information provided at the briefing on Solar One and was hoping that what the young warriors were about to see would not dissuade their courage before dropping onto the alien surface.

But, the Admiral had commanded all leaders to be totally transparent about what their soldiers would face. The lieutenant surveyed their faces; they were staring in anticipation.

"Okay, Team Four, welcome to your final training."

There was the traditional cheer from the soldiers and a few slaps on the back, as teams of athletes often did.

Sardo jumped up and yelled out. "YEAH, lock and load! Let's go wipe out that alien infestation!"

Among the cheers another soldier laughingly added, "Wait, we forgot the bug spray!" More cheers and laughter followed.

Sergeant Fuegal stood up. "ALRIGHT, that's enough, quiet down! Those *insects*, as you call 'em, own that planet and they can put you in a body bag quicker than you can squeeze the trigger. So, listen up, we've still got some serious training to do here.

"The perfect situation would be for us to get in and neutralize their weapons without engaging even one hostile alien. Unfortunately, that is not realistic. So, we'll see how much wiping-out you can do when some ugly alien sticks a weapon in your face. Remember what I taught you in Basic Training; it's what General Dayson and I both learned on that communications relay station. When you encounter the enemy, it will be the decisions you make in the first few moments that will determine your survival. Good-natured camaraderie is fine but it is no substitute for solid training." He motioned for the LT to continue.

The lieutenant felt slightly embarrassed that he had not been more serious with the soldiers, but he dismissed the feeling, figuring that the Sarge was better at the father-figure role.

"Sergeant Fuegal is right; this is serious business. First let me bring you up to date on the latest information about our mission. You have known for several Star Dates that Federation probes picked up evidence of atomic-based weapons on this alien planet. We know theirs is an older technology, the same as we had hundreds of Star Dates ago, but this species has developed them near the point of planet-destroying capability.

"The Federation is convinced that we have to act now before these creatures figure out how to complete the development of these weapons and find a way to deliver them off of their planet and possibly to other solar systems."

Ganz raised his hand. "Sir, can these weapons really destroy a whole planet? Or, is this just Federation hype?"

"No, Private, they can't quite destroy a

planet, not yet, but their technology is getting very close; it's only a matter of time."

The LT activated the video projection unit. A large hologram of a sphere appeared, floating and rotating just above the floor. The team stood and gathered around it.

"Here is a depiction of their planet. As you can see, it looks a lot like ours; it's also the third planet from their sun. However, theirs is farther out in its orbital plane, which accounts for the frigid temperatures we'll encounter on their planet's surface. The ambient temperature in our target area will be three times as cold as we're used to facing; about fifty temperature units difference. In addition to body armor we'll have to wear full cold weather survival suits.

"Also, the oxygen content of the atmosphere is so low we wouldn't last long without breathing gear."

Anson stared at the multicolored planet. "But Sir, how are we supposed to fight with all of that equipment on? And aren't we also going to wear our Personal Shield Generators? They can stop most laser blasts, right?"

"That's normally true but," He glanced at Sgt. Fuegal, "I'm sorry to have to tell you, but they won't work here. This planet's magnetic field is at a level three magnetism; it will mute our shield generators' effectiveness."

Fuegal added. "Listen, all of you, as soldiers you do what you have to do and wear what you have to wear to engage the enemy. We didn't have personal shield generators the last time I fought. If you don't have shields you just make sure your aim is good and that you take out the enemy before he has a chance to engage you. When you fight on the enemy's home turf you have to adjust. You've trained in this gear. Sure, it won't be a picnic but if you focus on your mission the supplemental stuff won't matter."

Sardo was smiling. "Sarge, just get me on the surface and turn me loose."

Fuegal glared for a moment. "Private, we train as a team and we fight as a team. Going solo might work in school or with females but out here in a hostile solar system it will most likely get your carcass a ticket home and a free Federation funeral."

Sardo knew he had struck a nerve. "Sure, I know Sarge, it was just a figure of speech." He thought for a moment. "When Team Four hits the surface what's it gonna be like anyway?"

The lieutenant touched his controller and the hologram zoomed in, showing the detailed topography of the alien world. "The surface has about the same variety of landscapes as most temperate planets, just a lot colder. Like many other planets in the galaxy it has vegetation, arid areas and large repositories of both frozen and liquid water.

"As I rotate this hologram, note the areas highlighted in red; those are the storage sites of their weapons. There are just over two hundred of these sites around the planet and they are all on land; we won't have to deal with water except in areas where rivers pass near targets. Altogether the Fleet has five hundred attack teams, so multiple teams will be working together.

"We will be landing with Attack Team Seven and our own Medical Unit. Team Seven will be on our right flank. The Fleet will have about a hundred teams in reserve, orbiting over the targets. We will be able to call for help on a moment's notice, if needed."

He zoomed in on one of the red dots. He reached in and touched the holographic image, and then spread his fingers apart. The image opened up to reveal the details of a large fenced-in area replete with what looked like rectangular storage buildings. There was a double row of fencing around it and towers on each corner, most likely staffed by alien guards.

The detail was not sufficient to determine the type of defensive weapons the creatures might wield. The soldiers stared in silence, trying to figure out how they could successfully attack such a target.

Sardo spoke first. "So, the gunships are going to prep the area with bombs or laser cannons before we attack, right?"

The lieutenant paused. "Well, no, they're not."

Sardo expressed the shock on all of the soldiers' faces. "What?! You're kidding aren't you, uh, sir? I mean, that's standard attack strategy, isn't it?"

"Yes, normally, but there are an untold number of old atomic-based weapons stored there. We can't be sure that bombs or laser cannons won't detonate them or at least break them apart and scatter material around that could contaminate the area. We and the aliens both are carbon-based life forms. Either result of such a strike could kill us as well as them. Going in with standard hand-held weapons is our only option."

Borta had been quiet up until now. He didn't want his new status to be common knowledge, just yet. He was still convinced that this whole operation was unnecessary, a colossal waste of time and Federation resources.

His biggest concern was that there would be loss of life, on both sides. His medical training and his recurring wayward dream during Deep Sleep had resulted in his increased passion for preserving life, even alien life. But, he had no clue how he would ever deal with what he was sure must be a grotesque alien anatomy.

He stepped closer to the lieutenant. "Sir, maybe the translation computers were able to decipher the alien language. Maybe the Admiral will negotiate with the aliens and we can all just go home."

The lieutenant was shaking his head. "I was hoping for that too but at the briefing on Solar One he told us the translation has not been successful. They haven't translated enough to even make contact with the aliens."

When the LT finished, the sergeant stepped forward and raised his left arm to Borta. There was a deep reddened scar running the entire length. "You see this scar, Private? I got this in the little alien skirmish we had some forty Star Dates ago on an outer spiral arm communications relay station.

"It happened right after the rogue planet military commander negotiated an end to the standoff. We were approaching the station for the agreed-to meeting and flew into an ambush. Fortunately, Lieutenant Dayson detected their intentions and we launched a surprise attack. She and I were both wounded but we overpowered the enemy force and recaptured the station.

"I had just gotten promoted from Private, just like you, and was a new Corporal in charge of a Squad. We let down our guard and were almost taken in by the ambush that was waiting for us.

"The alien planet leaders were just playing a political game, like most inhabited planets play. They were hoping we would back down and let them keep the relay station, which was Federation property and an essential communications link to the planets in that outer arm of the galaxy.

"So, as a result of that combat operation I made three decisions. First, I always want to be in Kate Dayson's Command. Second, I will never let my guard down again. And, third, my negotiation policy will continue to be, *keep your weapon armed and never trust an alien.*"

The soldiers were just staring at the sergeant; no one knew what to say. Their fear of their first combat was somewhat abated by their admiration of this experienced combat soldier and their new confidence of his Attack Team leadership.

Finally, Lieutenant Danade seized control of the training again. "The Admiral will tell everyone the instant he succeeds in any negotiations with these aliens. However, like I said, as of today our language computers have been unable to translate more than a few percent of the alien language. Our Intelligence experts are not hopeful that we will be able to communicate with these creatures on any significant level at all. So, for now, let's get back to our attack strategy."

"Sir?" Anson was staring at the planet's image. "What about the aliens themselves? Do we know what they look like and how their language sounds? And what kind of weapons will we be facing?"

The young leader hesitated a moment, glancing at the combat-hardened sergeant. Fuegal nodded to the LT, who then deactivated the image of the planet. He looked around the circle at his troops.

"What you are about to see is a life-sized image of what we believe to be a mature alien soldier, one you can expect to see in the target area. You may be concerned at first but just listen to the details before drawing any conclusions."

Having said that, he activated the control and a holographic image of an alien soldier appeared, floating and rotating just above the floor of the Battle Deck. Most of the soldiers recoiled from the image, some letting out gasps.

The alien before them stood three times larger than any soldier there. It had very long legs and gangly arms that branched out near the ends; their functions were unclear. Its body was chunky, with a somewhat bloated abdomen area. Its head seemed the most frightening; about four times larger than it should have been, its exaggerated circumference attached to the end of a thick neck, like a grotesque gnarled knob, mostly covered in what appeared to be a uniform layer of off-color secretion or growth of some kind.

Borta was astonished. "I've seen that alien before!"

Everyone was staring. The Sarg stepped closer. "What do you mean, you've seen it before? This image was just created by Intel. Are you crazy?"

Borta felt Anson's elbow in his side. He swallowed hard and recovered. He didn't want to have to describe the *dream* again, especially not to the whole team. "Ah...I mean this is kinda like what I imagined they would look like."

Sardo helped divert the attention back to the hologram. He had not recoiled from the sight but had actually stepped closer, inspecting the head and shoulders of this creature. He pointed out the myriad of strange openings that seemed to permeate portions of its head. He looked at the LT. "I'll go with Anson's question; do we know what this thing sounds like?"

"Yes, just give me a moment." The LT checked the notes on the small view panel. "The image you see is a composite of many images recorded by several probes. The accuracy is considered to be ninety percent. We have no details about what functions are served by the many openings you see on the alien's head. We assume they have something to do with communicating and perhaps feeding but we don't know why those functions would require so many orifices.

"Federation archives have no records of other creatures that resemble this one. Some of the openings may be for visual recognition during mating rituals or function as defense mechanisms but we can't be sure. Some may emit radar-type pulses for nonverbal communication. Intel feels certain that these creatures have no body shield-generation capabilities."

Most of the team had now moved closer for a detailed look at the creature.

The Lieutenant continued. "Now I'll play the sound of an alien audio transmission picked up by our probes." He pressed a control and the audio came out of the speakers. It was the most hideous sound they had ever heard. The aliens' voices seemed diabolical and almost sinister; what most would associate with evil. The tones were on the low end of the frequency spectrum and caused even the floor to vibrate. The soldiers got cold chills just listening. Finally, the transmission stopped. There was a moment of silence as the soldiers looked at each other.

Ganz injected a little levity. "So, we just won't ask them any questions and they won't do any talking, if talking is what that actually was." A few soldiers laughed nervously.

Sergeant Fuegal stepped closer. "Listen, these things definitely look ugly and they sound ugly, but we are the ones who can take them down; you are trained for it! They are carbon-based and as fragile as we are. That means they have some sort of liquid circulating through their bodies that will most likely leak out if wounded. It may even be toxic so avoid contact after you shoot one.

"Your primary aiming point should be the middle of the upper body. Your secondary point should be that ugly head. Just pull the trigger and put a few more laser holes in it."

All of the soldiers cheered and yelled, "Yeah!"

Sardo chimed in. "They look ugly and I'll bet they smell ugly too."

The LT was nodding. "Actually, you're right. Our probes sensed a distinct and disgusting odor associated with gatherings of these aliens. Less odor was detected in unpopulated areas.

"Fortunately, due to the low oxygen atmosphere we will be wearing breathing gear, so the pungent odor should not be a factor. However, we don't want to bring the odor back to our orbiting ships. So, the Environmental Division has set up decontamination stations in all air locks to clean our shuttles and battle suits when we return.

"Notice that this creature has some sort of colorful exoskeleton covering on its body. We have to assume it is some sort of body armor although we haven't determined if it is artificial or organic to each creature. Truth is; there's a lot we just don't know for sure.

"As far as weapons go, tactical analysis indicates theirs to be older technology but similar to ours, mostly older laser-based systems. But, be careful; their weapons can put a hole in you in an instant. Intelligence detected both hand-held and shoulder fired weapons. We have no data on their accuracy or effectiveness."

There was a long pause as each soldier tried to grasp the significance of the image hovering before them. Ganz stepped up by Sardo. "So, we are supposed to go up against weapons of unknown effectiveness, shoot our way past a bunch of these ugly smelly things, which will probably be ticked off at us, and then uncover the exact location of their planet-busting weapons? Uh...Okay...piece of cake! But what happens after that?"

The lieutenant cleared his throat. "Well, we need to locate and expose the weapons and atomic material so the two specialists from Chemical can get to them. They will be dropping with us and backpacking in the containers of Plonezite Neutralizer. As you recall from Basic Training, Plonezite, in the proximity of atomic material, neutralizes it at the subatomic level. When sprayed on containers of the material it will penetrate any casing and interact with the atoms, adding protons to the molecules and changing them into inert material."

Some soldier from the back questioned. "But, isn't Plonezite dangerous to carbon-based species, even us?"

"Yes, it is. That's why none of you can be anywhere near those weapons during the application of the neutralizer; our breathing systems can only filter out about half of the Plonezite molecules. The Chemical team will be wearing special protective gear for that purpose.

"For those of you concerned about the welfare of the aliens," There was laughter from the team, except from Borta, "the dangerous effects of Plonezite last only a short time. By the time we complete our withdrawal to the shuttle pickup sites the contamination should not be a factor.

"We are planning for the element of surprise to catch the aliens off guard, reducing actual combat action and casualties on both sides, although most of us won't lose a lot of sleep over a few dead aliens."

Most of the team cheered.

"Okay, that's it."

Sergeant Fuegal called them to attention. "Everybody, collect your gear and proceed to the Hologram Generator at the far end of the Battle Deck. We will meet Team Seven there for training. Since we will be in the first wave to hit the surface we have the first time slot for attack training.

"The Hologram Generator has been programmed with exact representations of the approach through the planet's atmosphere and the landing near our target. When you drop out of the shuttle into that hologram you will believe you are actually there.

"General Dayson has designed the sequence to be the most realistic training you've ever had. We will have six of their planet's rotations for training before we do our final preparations. Are there any questions before we go?"

Anson was not reassured by the sergeant's upbeat pitch. "Yeah, I have a question for Lieutenant Danade. Sir, a moment ago you mentioned that we hope to catch them by surprise. How is that possible? First of all, if they have very much space technology at all, they are sure to spot the whole Fleet zooming into their Solar System. We will be approaching at Level One Star Drive, right? That alone creates an ion trail that is easy to spot. And, we'll create a lot of fireballs when the shuttles' heat shields glow on approach through their atmosphere."

The LT nodded. "Of course we will eventually slow to shuttle launch speed but, yes, we will be approaching at Level One. However, the Admiral is using a new deception technique for solar system penetration. It's called Planet Shadowing.

"The computers were programmed to bring us out of the wormhole at the edge of their system when and where the planets here are most aligned to shadow us from detection. We will not be approaching directly but rather in more of an elliptical pattern, going from planet to planet, staying in their shadows.

"When we finally appear from behind their fourth planet we will be arrayed in a random formation, mimicking a meteor shower. The Admiral feels that, at least at first, the shuttles penetrating their atmosphere will seem like one of the many meteor showers this planet experiences. By the time they notice the difference it will be a very short time before each shuttle touches down in its target area, with little time for the aliens to coordinate a response."

After a short pause the Sarge took control again. "Okay, warriors! Move out!"

Chapter 8

Homesick

The *wake-up* tone roused the soldiers from sleep. Anson could smell the aroma of their morning ration of food being prepared in the Galley. He closed his eyes for a moment to remember what morning food was like back home. The ship's cooks did a decent job with mission rations but the soldiers always complained that the food was *not like home*. Although he seldom voiced such things, Anson had to agree with the complainers.

This was scheduled to be another grueling day of hologram training. He didn't understand why they had to repeat the sequence so many times. Maybe it was because of Sardo. Two training cycles ago he had missed the indications of danger and stepped on that simulated anti-personnel mine. Anson couldn't blame him. When the hologram generator projected that big ugly alien into the scene Sardo had jumped off of the cleared path rather than engage the enemy from where he stood. The Sarge had raked him over the coals for being in too much of a hurry; of not paying attention. His inattention, in real life, would have killed half of the Attack Team.

When the second wakeup tone sounded Anson placed his feet on the cold floor and stood to join the thousands of other soldiers in their morning preparation ritual. Anson smiled at the moaning and groaning of the soldiers who verbally dreaded another hard day of training. He thought it was dumb to keep complaining about something that was out of your control.

As Anson's Attack Team lined up in the passageway, waiting their turn to enter the dining area they saw a few soldiers exiting. They were all carrying large boxes and laughing together.

When they walked by, Ganz stopped one of them and asked. "Hey, what's in the boxes?"

The soldier kept walking slowly, "It's a surprise. Everybody gets a surprise." And then he ran to catch up with his friends.

The Team just looked at each other, puzzled. When they entered the area there were hundreds of boxes stacked on tables around the outer walls. A sign on a pedestal at the entrance said, *"Find the box with your name and take it to your place at the table."*

Everyone on the Team hurried to the table marked for Attack Team Four and searched for their individual box. Each one had a note affixed to the outside, which read, *"This box was packed by your family as a surprise for you, to be opened after arrival in the mission area. Admiral Platz has declared a Half-Rest for this training cycle. After your meal take some time off and enjoy the surprise your family has provided. The Training Alert System will notify you when it is time to report for the continuation of training."*

"Hey, look at this!" Sardo was holding up a model of an old Series 'B' Star Ship Fighter. "It's my favorite; I've had it hanging in my room for many star dates. I didn't even notice my Mother had sneaked it out. I fought off many attacking alien War Birds in my room with this thing." He was beaming with pride.

Each soldier was eating with one hand while digging through their box with the other. The first thing Anson saw in his box was the blue velvet neck pillow with Yanti's initial on it. She had used it as a decoration for her bed. She used to bring it out to the grassy area behind her house when they would lie there, looking up at the incredible galaxies and stars twinkling in the night sky. Anson enjoyed the closeness of sharing the pillow with her on those nights. He held it up to his nose and took a breath; he could smell her fragrance. He was caught up in the memory and hadn't noticed the other soldiers watching.

Ganz was the first to open the levity. "Well, well,...look what we have here; a pretty little velvet pillow. Maybe they should make it standard issue for all soldiers."

Sardo joined in. "Oh, my, if I had a pillow like that all I would want to do is sleep. I think Warrior Anson here will be pretty much worthless for the rest of the training."

Ganz added through his laughter. "You mean more worthless than he already is?"

Anson blushed a little, but smiled with them. "You love-starved losers would never understand. The only thing you've ever gotten from a female is *rejection*!"

Ganz and Sardo looked at each other. Ganz smiled and said, "Yep, he's pretty much right." They all laughed.

After they finished the meal they all left to enjoy the break from training in their own way. Anson took the box straight to his sleeping cube to survey the contents in more detail. There were several containers of various treats. His favorite was the batch of special flat round disks made from a mixture of Yantillian flax and fruit jelly. These were dried and preserved, making them last long periods of time. Anson had taken them on many camping trips.

There was his favorite lounging-around shirt, although there had been no time for *lounging* since they came out of Deep Sleep. He found a few other odds and ends and some sweet treats from some of the younger ones in the family. Inside was also a portable electronic data recorder which contained a mixture of voice recordings and text notes of encouragement from family members.

He was disappointed that there was no data message from Yanti. He thought that there must be some mistake; surely she would know how important a message from her would be. He moved everything around in the box, looking for another recorder that might have her message.

In the very bottom of the box he found an actual *paper* envelop. Inside was a hand-written love note from Yanti. His grandmother used to say that if someone wants to say something really important, they need to physically write it down. That way, no magnetic accident could erase what you had said. This was his first handwritten note since his grandmother had hand-written one to him when he entered school as a child. Anson gently opened the paper envelop and removed the note. He read it several times and smiled each time, imagining their future together.

Finally he took his favorite shirt out of the box and put it on. He then put the box aside and laid down on his bunk to write an electronic reply. This would be equally surprising to Yanti and others back home. After some contemplation he began entering data.

Dear Yanti,

I'm onboard Solar Two with over a thousand others but I have never felt more alone. I'm on my bunk, shut up in my sleeping cubicle so I can think and rationalize what we are about to do, and take time to prepare this message to you.

I must say I was pretty shocked to see that the Fleet had arranged for families to ship those surprise boxes with us on this mission. It was a great surprise to have it waiting when I went for our meal. We were all exhausted from the training regimen General Dayson designed to get us ready for combat, so getting the box and some extra time off was what we needed to give us an emotional shot in the arm.

Tell my mother that I really appreciate my

favorite shirt; I'm wearing it right now. The treats she sent won't last long, especially if the others find out that I have them. But, my favorite things in the box were your pillow, which is under my head at this moment, and your hand written letter. I knew that your grandmother had taught you how to do that but I never expected to get such a special communication from you. That really meant a lot.

I know you're wondering how you got this data chip so quickly, with us being ten star systems away. Well, this is where I get to surprise you. It's a new thing; this is the first mission to use it.

Fleet designed a Cargo Probe with a new hybrid-antimatter engine that can travel at Level Ten Star Drive through wormholes. Someday they may be able to take larger ships with troops on board through at that speed. The probe will be carrying all of the records for this mission, recorded on Master Chips for archiving back at Fleet Headquarters. If the mission ships suffer a major loss, the records will still be intact. The Admiral has also allowed all soldiers to send these data chips to loved ones back home. It's part of their Family Support Plan, just like the box you sent to me.

By the time you access this I will either be dead or on my way back home. I don't mean to shock you but that is the reality; anything can happen in combat. Either way, you won't know for sure until we come out of the Hole on your end, about a Star Date from now. Sorry for the uncertainty. I will do everything I can to survive this battle. But, if I am not successful I want you to know that the last thoughts I'll have on that planet's surface will be of you.

The main purpose of this data chip is to say that I am as committed to you as when you first said YES. You've had plenty of time to plan for our union so I am certain that you and your mother have done a great job. Surely, it will be a ceremony to remember. Ganz has agreed to stand up with me. I'm guessing he and Sardo have some sort of plans to do something unexpected to our travel shuttle after the ceremony so I'll have to be on the lookout for that. They enjoy playing practical jokes.

Borta has really changed; I don't think he'll

be at the ceremony. Right after coming out of Deep Sleep he declared himself to be a conscientious objector. (Be sure NOT to mention it to his family.) He had some sort of crazy dream that intruded in the middle of his Dream Chip and scared him into believing it is wrong to fight the aliens, even though their weapons threaten our system's planets. He is still going to the surface with us but he refuses to carry a weapon. I think he's a little crazy, not wanting to defend himself. But, who am I to judge?

I'm looking forward to life after the Fleet. You'll remember that at first I agreed to consider your Father's offer for you and me to move to Zorgon and for me to join his staff as an assistant at the Federation Headquarters, but I have decided against it. This mission has had a real impact on me, so much so that I don't want anything to do with politics right now—maybe later.

We have been training hard for the mission. General Dayson runs a thorough training system, which has had us in the Hologram Chamber often for the last six planet rotations.

We've practiced every tiny detail of the attack, over and over. I feel quite confident that I can do the job and that we will be successful enough to come home safe. The leaders are convinced that the alien species will be unable to threaten any Federation planet when we finish our mission. Although I have some moral concerns about all of this, there is a certain pride at being a part of doing something for a moral cause. After all, what we're doing will make the Universe safer for everyone--"

Anson stopped entering data. He saw an overhead light flicker and felt an unusual vibration. Then his body began slowly sliding toward the foot of his bed. He knew immediately that it was the deceleration phase that had forced him to move toward the foot rail. Solar Two was slowing to shuttle launch speed. He lifted his Data Entry Pad back onto his lap and continued his thought.

...especially our families back home.

Well, I just now felt the ship begin decelerating so the shuttles will be able to launch, which is planned for about a planet-rotation from now. I just want to get this mission over with so I can see you again. Fleet will alert all of the families when we exit the Galactic Four back near home, which should give you plenty of time to get a party ready and meet me at the shuttle port. I can hardly wait to see the smile on your beautiful face.

Be sure to Data Feed this to my parents and tell them not to worry. Give them my love. Remember, you are the light of my life! The images of you stored in my feeble brain are keeping me focused on doing this job well. Until our homecoming I am; YOURS!

Love...Anson

Anson removed the chip from the data recorder and secured it in the small metal storage envelop. He then marked it with Yanti's name and address. As he stared at the envelop it occurred to him that he had not actually contemplated what would happen to his family and Yanti if he did *not* make it through the coming attack.

Other family members, usually the older

ones, had died before and, after some grief, the family had moved on with their lives. But he couldn't remember any young ones ever dying. He couldn't wrap his mind around the possibility of actually losing his life. He supposed that Yanti would eventually find someone else to love and they would become one and live happily ever after. He shuddered a little, not wanting to continue that thought.

Anson knew that the Cargo Probe would launch into the Hole as soon as launch speed was reached so he headed toward Lieutenant Danade's office with his *surprise* for Yanti.

As he hurried out into the passageway he almost bumped into Sardo. His friend just barely jumped out of the way in time.

"Hey, lover-boy, you're in a big hurry." Sardo noticed the envelop in Anson's hand. "So, you been writing the *Farewell Darling* letter to Yanti? Don't worry buddy; if you don't make it, I will be sure to give her a shoulder to cry on. And if she needs more than that, well, I'll be there for her." He could hardly contain his laughter.

Anson gave him a playful punch in the gut. "Yeah, I'll bet you would. That's about the only way you'd ever get a female to get close to you." They both laughed.

Anson held up the envelop. "Actually, this is an encouragement message to her. I told her not to worry and that everything would work out just fine. I told her basically that the mission is just routine and that we are ready to do the job and come home."

Sardo stopped and stared for a moment. "I'm glad you believe that because I feel the same way. I just wish everybody on the Team was as confident as we are."

They both walked together to the next cross-passageway and then parted directions. Anson walked down the adjacent passageway to Lieutenant Danade's office and handed the Message Chip to him.

As the officer took the envelop he smiled and said, "Nice shirt."

Anson looked down, realizing he had forgotten to take it off. The Battle-Ready uniform was expected outside of personal spaces.

Before he could make an excuse the LT held up his hand and shook his head. "Don't worry about it, this time." He added Anson's envelop to those already in the desk drawer and then smiled. "I hope your data message gives her confidence. You have every reason to be so."

Anson half-smiled. "I feel I'm ready, sir. I'll do my job if you'll do yours."

The LT smiled and stuck out his hand. "Agreed."

Chapter 9

The Attack

Admiral Platz had his final meeting with all of his combat leaders. His report that the Translation Division had been unsuccessful confirmed the rumors everyone had heard. He had each of his Support Commanders give their final instructions to the combat leaders.

The Admiral was confident that the mission would be successful. General Dayson reported that the onboard training had been more successful than expected. Having such intensive realistic training just prior to the attack had honed the soldiers' skills to a fine edge. The General was prepared to make such training a standard fare on all future missions.

On all three Fleet ships there was a whirlwind of activity. Laser weapons were charged up and checked. Shuttles were fueled and supplies were loaded. No one slept. Medical teams did their final search and rescue drills in the Hologram Chamber.

The staffs of onboard hospitals met to

practice all possible contingencies. Doctors studied the composite of the aliens' bodies, trying to devise a plan for medics to treat any of them that may become wounded and surrender to an Attack Team.

On Solar Two a thousand soldiers loaded their personal combat gear onto their shuttles and then reported to the dining area for their final special meal before the attack. No expense had been spared. The spread was the most delicious food any of them could remember. They ate like the Emperor of the Federation.

The conversations among soldiers remained jovial and mostly avoided the uncertainties that many felt. Anson felt ready but there was still that *something* in the pit of his stomach he couldn't quite resolve.

Following the meal, all Attack Teams assembled on the Battle Deck for a special address. General Dayson had chosen to personally give the traditional pep-talk to the soldiers on Solar Two.

All eyes were on her because of her commanding presence, standing on the

Command Platform in full Battle Dress. The soldiers were astounded that the General had elected to personally oversee the attack from the Command Shuttle of their Attack Battalion. Her speech was short and to the point. When she finished every soldier was ready to hit the planet's surface full speed and get the job done.

Finally, the Ready Light overhead in the center of the Battle Deck illuminated. The computer made the announcement. *"All combat personnel, don your combat equipment and report to your shuttles. Prepare for launch."*

All soldiers proceeded to the storage bays where their survival equipment and weapons were waiting. They used the *buddy method* to help each other into the cumbersome battle suits and environmental systems. Even after the extensive hologram training in these uniforms, some felt too restricted to be totally effective as soldiers. But all felt ready to do what had to be done.

Anson's heart was almost beating out of his chest as he climbed aboard the attack shuttle and strapped into his seat. Ganz was telling jokes, trying to lighten the moment. Sardo was his usual gung-ho self, ready to charge the target. Borta was somber-faced while securing the last of the medical gear. The lieutenant was the last one on. He counted heads and keyed his communicator.

"Team Four present and accounted for; ready to launch."

That same message was transmitted to Operations by hundreds of other lieutenants. When all shuttles had reported in, the onboard communications systems activated.

The Admiral spoke. "This is Admiral Platz. You are about to embark on an historic mission, the first of its kind in the Federation's history. I am proud of every one of you. You are the Federation's finest! You are the best trained, best equipped force ever assembled.

"As you know by now, we were unable to establish effective communications with this planet's species. So, as you begin this mission, rest assured that your leaders are motivated and professional and I have no doubt that they, and each of you, will do your duty. While you are on the surface be sure to focus on the mission. Watch out for each other. Remember, as always, we leave no warrior behind.

"It seems that our attempt at stealth has been successful to this point. There's no reason to believe our deception as a meteor shower in their atmosphere will not work as well."

The Admiral hesitated. "I expect all leaders to keep the safety of your soldiers as a top priority. I'm ordering all of you to come back safe. Stay safe!"

The red lights on all shuttles began flashing. The computer counted down to zero and the green lights illuminated. Team Four's shuttle vibrated as the interior was pressurized. It came to a hover and moved aft, into the massive air lock.

Once the first wave of fifty shuttles was inside, the inner doors closed and the outer pressurized panels slowly opened, revealing a breath-taking view of the alien solar system, with the multicolored target planet filling most of the view. The multiple shuttle launches were timed to look like a large meteor that was breaking up into smaller ones. The meteor-shower ruse was working.

Team Four's soldiers, crowded together in the cramped shuttle, had a birds-eye view of the looming planet out through the pilots' cockpit glass panel.

The environmental system couldn't stem the flow of perspiration on Anson's face or soothe the nauseating lump in the pit of his stomach. He knew that soldiers throughout the eons of history had experienced such sensations when they first went into battle.

He closed his eyes to do some final mental preparation. Soon, the craft began to vibrate violently. The g-forces pressed him deeper into his seat and his face began to feel hot and flushed. His helmet became uncomfortably tight and his head felt heavy. He opened his eyes to see fire engulfing the shuttle. They were entering the planet's atmosphere.

Chapter 10

The Aliens

After dinner, little Julie was lying on the picnic blanket spread out on the soft grass in her back yard. She was watching the night sky from their country home in upstate New York. Suddenly, her eyes widened and she pointed up.

"Mommy, look! Is that another meteor shower?"

Her mother looked up and smiled. "Sure is, honey. It's beautiful, isn't it?"

THE END

ABOUT THE AUTHOR

Max Holt is a retired U.S. Army pilot, having served 22 years on active duty including two combat tours in Vietnam. He is also a retired minister who served two different congregations over a 15 year period. Max is an avid Science Fiction reader and writer. This work is one of several to be published under Max's publishing company, Max Holt Media.

Max has two sons and six grandchildren. He is retired and lives in Mount Juliet, Tennessee.

Additional titles published by Max Holt Media include:

"THE DOME," Book One in the A.I. RISING Series by Max Holt

"UNDERNEATH THE MOON" Series, Books 1 through 6, by Dan Holt and Max Holt

"SLEEP MODE" and "KEEPSAKE" by Dan Holt

All are available at www.amazon.com.